This delicious woman was trying to seduce him!

Zach and Jenny were sitting very close now, and Jenny was running her hand back and forth on his chest in the same provocative way she'd caressed his thigh. There was no disguising the fact that his jeans were becoming more and more uncomfortably tight.

"I'll just pull this out . . ." Jenny was tugging on his T-shirt now, pulling it out of the waistband of his jeans.

Zach was mesmerized. This was about to become a full-scale seduction.

" . . . And slip my hands up under here. . . . Mmm, your skin feels so good, Zach."

She moved so that her breasts were pressed against him, rubbing against his chest with slow, sinuous movements.

His breathing grew erratic. No one had ever aroused his passions more than Jenny. She was so tempting . . . but it wouldn't work. They were just too damn different.

And then Jenny kissed him and his doubts left him . . . for now.

Each of **Bobby Hutchinson**'s romances contains bits and pieces contributed by whatever family member she manages to corner and question. The idea for *A Legal Affair* came from her daughter-in-law Trudy. When Trudy was studying law, she told Bobby fascinating tales about working in a legal-aid clinic in Vancouver, and patiently answered Bobby's millions of questions. When Bobby isn't writing romances, she teaches romance writing and is a dedicated runner, gourmet vegetarian and reader—currently of books on parapsychology. Bobby and her husband live in British Columbia.

Books by Bobby Hutchinson

HARLEQUIN TEMPTATION
285–STRICTLY BUSINESS

HARLEQUIN SUPERROMANCE
337–A PATCH OF EARTH
375–REMEMBER ME
443–JOURNEY'S END

A Legal Affair

BOBBY HUTCHINSON

Harlequin Books

TORONTO • NEW YORK • LONDON
AMSTERDAM • PARIS • SYDNEY • HAMBURG
STOCKHOLM • ATHENS • TOKYO • MILAN

For Trudy Hopman Jackart,
my lawyer, daughter-in-law and friend

Published November 1991

ISBN 0-373-25471-7

A LEGAL AFFAIR

1

"SO YOU'RE A LAWYER, right? I wanna know, what are my constitutional rights, here? How come parking meters only take quarters? Tell me *why* I should hafta carry around a pocketful of quarters when I've got dimes and nickels?"

A dirty fist plunged into a trouser pocket and came up with several coins.

"Just because they don't fit in the stupid machines, it's not my fault, right? And then some jerk up and tows my car! Is that *fair*, lady?"

Jenny Lathrop frowned at the bald giant scowling at her as he leaned against the narrow table that served as her desk.

"I ast you a question, lady lawyer. Answer me. You think tha's fair?"

Jenny pushed her wire-framed glasses higher on her nose, wishing that Vancouver's finest had towed Mr. Obnoxious away, instead of his car.

Jenny was beginning to believe that she'd made a big mistake, wanting to practice law. Here she was, a third-year student, donating valuable hours of her time to help people who couldn't afford to pay a practicing lawyer, and her very first client turned out to be a nut case.

Parking meters? Constitutional rights over whether the damned things took nickels and dimes? This wasn't exactly what she thought Professor Moffat had meant about people needing her advice.

"Working in the Legal Clinic will be a great experience," he'd enthused. "You work one-on-one with clients just the way you'll be doing when you're out in the field. The clinic's open once a week, on Thursday evenings beginning at seven sharp. There's always a graduate lawyer in attendance to help you with any problems."

Well, Jenny was having a problem, all right. She shot a glance across the room, hoping she could catch the eye of the graduate lawyer and get him to come over.

Mr. Jones was tall and elegant looking in his fancy three-piece suit. Jenny figured he was maybe thirty-four, thirty-five. At this moment he was bent solicitously over blond and curvaceous Gloria Spencer, one of Jenny's classmates. He had the same mesmerized look on his face that most of the male professors had whenever they were within a ten-foot radius of Gloria.

She recalled a comment a cynical friend of hers had made about why young lawyers volunteered for this job as clinic adviser.

"Sixty percent of law students are now female. Volunteering at clinics is a good way for these guys to meet women who are easily impressed by graduate lawyers. It ain't altruism that attracts them, honey."

And it didn't look as if she was going to have any luck getting Mr. Jones's attention away from Gloria. Jenny stared down at her neat piles of supplies on the table, hoping for inspiration. There were waivers, divorce kits, the *Law Student's Legal Advice Manual*, even a package of tissues in case some poor client burst into tears.

The way things were going, she might need the tissues herself.

She allowed herself one last, panicked glance at the Interview Checklist, page 1, point A.

Instructions for opening the interview: Greet client, make him feel comfortable, establish rapport by small talk, seat client, stress that client should carefully read the waiver and sign it....

The all-important waiver.

"Listen," she began again, raising her voice and trying to be patient. "I can't be of any help to you unless you sign this, Mr., uh, what did you say your name was?"

She leaned forward and shook the paper in an effort to get his attention, but quickly drew back. The smell of liquor on his breath was enough to give her a hangover.

"My name's none of your business. I'm here for legal advice, like the sign outside said, so don't you raise your voice to me. I got my rights. This here's the free legal-advice clinic, ain't it? So give me some free advice, Red."

Red wasn't exactly her favorite nickname. Being teased about her copper-colored hair always raised every hackle in Jenny's body.

Free clinic or not, she was a professional and expected to be treated like one. Furious, she got up from her chair and leveled her most lethal glare at him.

"You've had too much to drink, that's what I figure. And you won't listen to a single word I say. So if you're going to go on with this monologue, then I suggest you leave," she ordered in a shaky, high voice.

He sneered at her. "Well, hoity-toity, aren't we? Who the hell are you to order me around?"

"That's it. Out you go, right now. Get out. As far as I'm concerned, this interview is over."

He stuck out his bulldog jaw at her and gave her an evil grin.

"Is that so?" he snapped, and then smashed a meaty fist down on the table, sending neat papers flying in all directions. It was a wonder the table legs didn't collapse. The sound echoed through the large room, quieting the subdued buzz of the other nine law students and drawing horrified stares from their clients.

"Leave, huh? Well, we'll just see who the hell is leaving around here!" His voice filled the room.

Jenny flinched, her anger shifting to alarm. She suspected that this Neanderthal wouldn't hesitate to hit her next. What to do?

Her gaze slid past her client's massive bulk and noted that now help was on the way. The classily dressed Mr. Jones, Q.C., L.L.D., had finally noticed something was wrong. He was striding over to her desk, a frown on his face.

Relief spilled through her when he appeared at the giant's left shoulder.

He put a manicured hand on her client's forearm and inquired in a deep, cultured baritone, "What seems to be the problem here . . . ?"

As if it were happening in slow motion, Jenny saw the man's fist curl and a vicious snarl appear on his beefy red face. He swung at Jones and connected. Jones grunted and, staggering back, grabbed at a chair, missed, and fell heavily to the floor, as blood burst from his finely shaped nose.

Stunned, he lay still for a moment.

Several women screamed.

The giant guffawed.

Two male law students came rushing over and then hung back, apparently having second thoughts about tackling Jenny's burly client, who was now feinting with his fists like a prizefighter, his broad back toward her and his treelike legs braced against her table as if he planned to take on every man in the room.

Jones was struggling to get to his feet. He looked affronted, like a monarch who'd been slammed in the face by a common thug. More people were crowding around.

There were screams, and someone hollered, "Call the police!" But no one seemed to be doing anything practical.

Suddenly disgusted by the lack of positive action, Jenny grabbed the first heavy thing at hand. It happened to be her massive four-inch-thick, *University of British Columbia Law Student's Legal Advice Manual*. She stepped up on her chair and then onto the unsteady surface of the table. She raised the book as high over her head as she could, and brought it down on her client's bald pate with every ounce of strength in her slender body.

Though her tormentor's knees buckled, still he didn't go down. He grunted and looked slowly around and up at her with a comically amazed expression, and then swore loudly as three male students and two clients grabbed his arms and hustled him out the door. He didn't put up much resistance at all.

Jenny scrambled down from the tabletop.

Pandemonium reigned. Everyone talked at once.

"You gonna sue the guy, Mr. Jones?"

"You want us to call an ambulance? Does it feel like your nose is broken?"

"Hey, anybody manage to get that guy's name or an address?"

Three female students were hovering over Mr. Jones, who was now off the floor and sprawled on the chair in front of Jenny's desk, pressing a wad of bloody tissue to his nostrils.

As Jenny gaped at him, Jones's thick, dark eyebrows rose like haughty question marks over angry green eyes. He glared back at her. There was something so amusing about his outraged expression that Jenny had the urge to laugh.

She suppressed one hysterical giggle, and then another. She tried to look away from Mr. Jones but was unable to move an eyelash. She felt her face turning red and hot, and she just knew her freckles were standing out like beacons across her nose and on her cheeks.

Stop it, Jenny.

"What's your name?" His query was muffled by the tissues, but it was understandable.

She couldn't answer. Bubbles of laughter floated up in her like helium gas. His burning gaze impaled her. Well, he might as well make good use of his eyesight while it lasted. It would only be a matter of hours before both those disconcerting green eyes turned interesting shades of black and swelled almost shut—if her guess was worth anything.

Mr. Constitutional Rights had landed Jones a good one right on the button.

My, he certainly had long eyelashes for a man with such a livid stare. Long eyelashes, and a sort of... regal presence.

It's a wonder his blood isn't blue, she thought, as hysteria battled with good sense. If ever a man looked as if he ought to have blue blood, Jones did.

His wavy dark brown hair hung in disarray over his forehead, and the front of his vest and fancy pink shirt and his gray-and-blue striped silk tie were covered with large bloodstains. The impeccable light gray suit was rumpled and dusty, and his trouser knees were filthy.

"Mr. Jones, one of us will be glad to drive you to the hospital," a female student suggested, brushing reverently at the dirt on his sleeve.

He ignored the offer and the fussing. Instead, he steadily regarded Jenny's scarlet face.

"What... is your... name?"

She was going to have to answer.

"Jenny. Umm, Jenny Lathrop." She struggled for control, swallowed, shoved her glasses higher on her nose and managed to overcome her treacherous laughter. "I'm, umm, a third-year law student."

Now that she was up close to him, she saw that Jones wasn't any weakling. Even sitting down, she could tell he was tall—probably a good ten inches taller than her. And he had wide shoulders for a lawyer.

"Mind telling me what went on between you and our mutual friend?"

Jenny told herself not to be intimidated. He was only a man, after all. A good-looking man. Under other circumstances, he might even be... sexy?

Whacking that bum on the head must have affected her brain.

But he had a good shape for a lawyer—no denying that. No sign of spread or spillover in the parts that usually expanded when a guy got successful. And if that classy suit was any indication, Jones was doing fine in his practice.

Probably some nice, profitable, boring, safe, corporate specialty. The thought sobered her.

"Well . . . Ms. . . . Lathrop? I'm waiting for some sort of explanation."

There was every indication in his tone that she was trying what little patience he had left.

Jenny was well aware of that, and grew irritated. If he expected an apology, he was barking up the wrong tree. What had occurred here wasn't the result of a single thing she'd said or done. She was innocent.

"It . . . it certainly wasn't my fault, if that's what you're thinking," she said, her indignation causing her to stammer. "I, umm, he—that man—just wouldn't listen. He went on and on and wouldn't sign the waiver, and he insulted me, so I asked him to leave." She drew in a deep breath and pushed her glasses higher on her nose. "He was raving on about parking meters and constitutional rights and his car getting towed away." She paused and then frowned when it struck her that constitutional rights weren't covered in the legal-advice manual. "How come the rights aren't in the manual? I've never seen any sign of them, and I've read the blamed thing from front to back until I practically know it by heart."

Jones looked nonplussed, but only for a split second. "I have no idea, and it's irrelevant. Now, what else happened? In detail."

Trying to sound dignified through a wad of tissue was not easy, as Jones was discovering. Fresh blood was now seeping through the tissues, but he did pretty well under the circumstances.

Jenny spotted her own package of tissues on the floor near her feet and bent over to retrieve them. Then she yanked out a good dozen, walked around the desk and thrust them at Jones. He took them and smoothly replaced one set with the other without one word of thanks.

She could smell his after-shave, or cologne, or whatever it was he wore. It was clean and outdoorsy—a definite contrast to his disheveled state.

Boy, did he ever bleed! She'd hate to be around if he was really wounded.

"What exactly did you say to set him off, Ms. Lathrop?"

He certainly was persistent. And judgmental, as well. For pete's sake, he still seemed to think it was her fault.

Was she on trial here?

"How do I know what set him off? He was drunk, looking for a fight. When I told him that he ought to leave, he smashed his fist on the table. Then you came over, and he punched you out."

"I'm well aware of that segment of the incident." His voice dripped with sarcasm.

"Well, that's a relief."

She knew she sounded sharp, but darn it all, he'd asked for it. What did he expect—a full psychological workup on some crazed drunk?

Their gazes held in a silent battle of wills. Finally Jones became aware that clients and students were milling around in a general state of disorder, many of them eavesdropping on everything he and Jenny were saying.

"Okay, everybody, let's get back to work," he announced in an authoritative way, and to Jenny's surprise, people returned to their tables, clients took their places in chairs and soon the hum of quiet conversation again filled the room.

"You must be used to having the serfs obey." She was sorry the instant the words were out.

He ignored it, however, other than giving her one last, scathing look.

"I suggest you carry on, as well, Ms. Lathrop," he said after a long pause. "There're a lot of people waiting, and you've wasted a great deal of time already."

She'd wasted time? She got angry all over again, but it faded once Jones turned and headed for the door, probably to find the washroom.

Jenny felt a pang of sympathy as she watched him walk away. There was a huge dirt stain across the back of his jacket, and for some reason, he looked a lot more vulnerable from the back than he had from the front. He had a crazy cowlick at the crown of his head. And he also had a neat, tight bottom and strong, long legs.... Heat enveloped her and she suddenly felt weak in the knees. She collapsed onto her chair and drew in several deep breaths, wondering if there was a hope in hell that the rest of the evening was going to improve.

A FAT WOMAN wearing a cherry-red knitted hat pulled down tight over her ears must have been watching for Jenny to sit down before she came over. She looked forty or even fifty. Her brown raincoat was buttoned to the neck, and she sidled over and eased herself into the chair in front of Jenny's desk without removing either hat or coat.

Now, this time, let's get this right, Lathrop. Greet the client.

"Hello there. How are you this evening?" Jenny pasted a wide, phony smile on her stiff face, making a point of standing and holding her hand out in a welcoming way. The woman hesitated and then touched Jenny's hand with yellow nicotine-stained fingers and drew back as if the contact were electric. Her watery blue eyes didn't quite meet Jenny's gaze.

"I'm Jenny Lathrop, and . . . your name is . . . ?"

"Veronica. I'm Veronica Glickman, I been here lots before. I seen what you done to that bum just now, and I wanna say I think it was something. He was no gentleman, that's for sure. You know how to take care of yourself, and I like that in a woman. So I asked the girl at the door if I could come over to you." Her voice was rough and low-pitched, as if she smoked too much. There was an aura of toughness about her. There was also a pungent smell like rotting fruit.

Jenny instinctively wanted to move back out of the woman's immediate vicinity, but didn't. Instead she smiled, more naturally this time, and at last made eye contact with her client. Something in Veronica's eyes made her seem vulnerable.

"Well, Ms. . . . Glickman, thank you. And I'm delighted to be your counselor. Now, before we talk about your reason for coming here tonight, I must explain the purpose of this waiver. . . ."

It wasn't a perfect production, but it was the best Jenny had to offer at the moment. It was a thousand times better than her first disaster; that was certain.

Ten minutes later—waiver signed and over with—
Veronica began to relax. First, she tugged the knitted
cap off, revealing a brownish-gray mass of short hair
that looked as if it had been lopped off with garden
shears. She was talking all the while, complaining in a
disjointed fashion about the student she'd seen last time
she'd come to the Legal Clinic.

"See, I told him, I said I need a lawyer, somebody
smart, because the damn city is going to tear down my
house. Says so right here on this paper.... Now,
where'd I put it? But he didn't listen right, that boy
didn't. Said there wasn't anything he could do. Where
is that cussed paper, anyway?"

She launched a search through the pockets of her
raincoat, clicking her tongue against her teeth when she
didn't find what she was looking for.

Then, to Jenny's amazement, Veronica unbuttoned
the raincoat and revealed another, heavier coat underneath—this one a bright wool plaid, with a mad assortment of junk in the pockets, but not the paper
Veronica was looking for. She was becoming more and
more agitated, muttering under her breath, and her
hands were shaking.

More buttons were undone. Still another coat was
revealed, blue this time, and under that a heavy sweater
over a voluminous skirt. In the skirt pocket, Veronica
at last located a crumbled, soiled and multifolded letter, which she triumphantly handed to Jenny. She was
perspiring, and she accepted the tissue Jenny offered
and mopped her face with it.

"Here. I knew I brought it."

Jenny took the paper, saddened at what she'd seen.
Veronica wasn't fat at all. She was actually rather

scrawny under her protective covering. And Jenny suspected that she was also mentally disturbed.

Jenny unfolded the letter, which smelled like Veronica, and quickly scanned it.

It was a formal notice from the city Health Department stating that a house located at 4905 Powell Street was in the process of being condemned for health reasons.

"This is where you live, Veronica?"

"It's my house. I own that house. They got no right to tear it down. It's mine." A tear leaked out of the corner of her eye and found a path down the wrinkles on her cheek. She sniffed noisily. "Can you do anything?"

Jenny thought about it. There wasn't any way to check on the ownership of the property tonight. And the Health Department wouldn't open till nine tomorrow, either.

"Ms. Glickman, I can't help you right this minute, but I promise I'll have answers for you by next Thursday. I promise I'll do whatever is possible to help you. Can you come back and see me again at that time? This card has my name on it. You tell the aide at the door that you have an appointment with me."

"Sure. Sure, I'll be here Thursday, and you call me Veronica." She slid Jenny's card into some pocket or other, and began the laborious process of buttoning, zipping and tying all her various garments together again while Jenny filled in necessary details in a file with Veronica's name on it.

When she was done, Veronica yanked her cap down over her ears, waved a hand at Jenny and shuffled away.

THE OTHER CLIENTS Jenny had were straightforward. She didn't have to refer to the legal-advice manual even once. Her confidence returned. Once again sure of herself, she was filled with enthusiasm for her career in law.

She was in control.

She was only subliminally aware that Mr. Jones had never reappeared.

But he surfaced in her dreams that night.

BRENDA PENNINGTON was at her desk when Zachary Jones strode into his office at eight-fifteen Friday morning.

"Morning, Mr. Jones. You're early." Brenda had never succumbed to the informality of calling the partners by their first names.

Her lush blond exterior was a cover-up for the managerial skills and iron will of a thirty-year-old Margaret Thatcher. She'd been hired four years before. The partners had taken one look at her delicate face, lavish bosom and valentine-shaped bottom, and agreed unanimously.

"Hi, Brenda," Zach mumbled, doing his best to hold the morning paper at an angle that would cover his matched set of black eyes and swollen nostrils.

He'd hoped that maybe by coming in forty-five minutes before his usual arrival time, he'd escape just the sort of intensive scrutiny Brenda was now giving him. He should have known better.

"You get yourself in another brawl, Mr. Jones?"

Brenda had no illusions about any of the partners. She hadn't fallen for a single one of the furtive, but ingenious, carnal propositions each had made to her at some point over the past years. She treated them as if they were slow children, and accepted no excuses whatsoever as far as their productivity was concerned.

"Brenda, that's unfair. You make it sound as if I go out looking for recreational fights." Zach was in no mood for insinuations. "The only other time I had a black eye was when I fell off my board wind-surfing and the damn thing bashed into me."

"There was that wedding eight months ago, Mr. Jones."

"I was severely provoked on that occasion, Brenda." He tried to speak as haughtily as possible, but not being able to breathe through his nose made him sound adenoidal instead.

Brenda went on eyeing him with morbid curiosity.

"Is it broken?"

Zach was about to shake his head when he remembered how movement of any kind made his head feel.

"The doctor said probably cracked, but not needing a splint or realignment."

"Well, that's positive, isn't it?"

Zach could tell she wasn't finished yet.

"So what happened this time? How'd you get a matched set instead of a single?"

"A certifiable lunatic at the law clinic last night went berserk and socked me one."

"You get his name? We could sue on the grounds that you're going to scare customers away, looking like that."

Zach tried to scowl at her, but he knew from the sight that had greeted him in the mirror that morning that scowling was just as impossible as smiling. His face was both painful and frozen into one set expression.

"Not much point in suing somebody who goes to a free legal clinic," he growled. "Waste of time."

"Well, I wondered why you volunteered at that clinic in the first place. Altruism really doesn't suit you, Mr. Jones."

Before he could think of an answer to that, Zach heard the door open and shut behind him, and Ken Meredith's cheerful voice yodeled a good-morning.

Zach attempted a fast getaway. He'd had it up to the teeth with questions already this morning. There'd been the elevator man in his apartment building, the news vendor, the parking attendant . . . and Brenda.

He hurried toward the stairs leading to his second-floor office, with Ken dogging his heels like a terrier.

"Zach? Hey, Zach, old buddy. So, did you score at that clinic last night like we figured? Was it worth the time invested? Any lovely ladies old uncle Ken might connect with? Zach? Whadda ya say, hotshot?"

Ken's voice was growing blessedly fainter. Zach took the stairs to his office two at a time, doing his best to ignore the bolts of pain that shot through his head with each jarring step.

He didn't need to be reminded that his motives in volunteering at the damned legal-aid thing were a lot less than honorable, and he was furious with Ken for airing them in front of Brenda. He could imagine the knowing looks she was aiming at his back right this minute.

"So what's with him, Brenda? He get up on the wrong side of the bed, or what? I only asked a friendly question."

From the top of the landing, Zach heard Brenda giving his partner a rundown on his black eyes and swollen nose.

"It's quite grotesque. He's disfigured," he heard her comment, and Ken was unfeeling enough to guffaw.

Safe at last in his spacious office, Zach closed the door and moved toward the wall-size window where he stared unseeingly out, reviewing the past evening's events for the fiftieth time.

The thing that galled him was getting knocked down without even raising his fists.

If he hadn't still been fantasizing about that gorgeous blonde named Gloria something or other, maybe he'd have reacted quicker when that bastard socked him.

He sure as hell hadn't come off looking like any hero. The guy had coldcocked him when he least expected it. His lips tightened, and he was filled with rage. He'd give a lot for a chance to even the score.

And why the hell should the image of that skinny woman with those outdated wire-framed glasses and wild hair like new copper pennies keep intruding into his battered brain?

Had the punch on his nose dislodge some part of his mind? He could barely remember what the tall blonde looked like this morning, but every damned freckle on the redhead was etched in his memory.

He'd always gone for tall blondes, he reminded himself.

This girl . . . this Jenny Lathrop . . . Hell, she wasn't his type at all.

Not physically. Tiny, kind of flat-chested, wiry.

Not his type emotionally, either. She didn't have a shred of human kindness in her.

Strong, though. He remembered the gratifying sound of the blow she'd dealt the Neanderthal. Gutsy, when even the men were hanging back like wimps, letting the Neanderthal control the scene.

She had a fast, wicked mouth. He remembered women like her from his student days—always quick with an answer. Defensive. Antagonistic. Smart. Aggressive.

Interesting?

He recalled dating one or two. They'd made a nice change, driven him temporarily nuts and made him doubly grateful for the compliant cheerleader types.

Like Annemarie.

Was he getting old or stale or what? Since Annemarie walked out on him two months ago, he'd been uncharacteristically slow at finding a replacement.

Well, it wasn't going to be the likes of this redhead!

What sort of woman was she, anyway? What sort of woman would laugh when a guy was grievously injured, for God's sake?

And yet . . . There'd been that unmistakable current of pure energy running between them. Sexual energy.

Get ahold of yourself, Jones. She's nothing but trouble.

Look what happened to you the very first moment you were in her vicinity. You got socked in the face for no good reason. Now, wouldn't that seem a less-than-gentle hint from fate to stay away from that woman forever?

And yet, he kept remembering the damnedest things about her, when he least expected it. That uncontrollable grin, for one thing. God, that grin had gotten under his skin.

Other things, too. Eyes so very, very blue. She had a sort of triangular face, high cheekbones and a small, determined chin; and her nose was tiny, so those ridiculous glasses kept slipping down and needing to be pushed up again. She pushed at them with one clumsy index finger like a little kid might, and he'd found the gesture oddly endearing.

Then, from his undignified position on the floor, and with her up on that stupid table, he'd been forced to notice that her legs under that short black skirt were far too long and shapely to suit the rest of her. And there'd been a flash of pristine white panty when she—

The memory brought an undeniable surge in his groin.

But you're a bosom man, he reminded himself.

His intercom buzzed, and he sighed and moved to answer it.

He should have called in sick today. He didn't feel one hundred percent—in body or in spirit. He felt rather irritable and edgy and sore all over, and his sense of humor had gone on holiday without him.

"Mr. Jones," Brenda intoned, "there's a Ms. Jenny Lathrop on line one, wanting to speak with you. Also, your nine o'clock appointment is here a bit early. Should I send him up?"

Zach would never admit that a simple light blinking insistently on his telephone could have anything to do with a general lightening of his spirits or a significant rise in his blood pressure.

Without a doubt, Ms. Jenny Lathrop was calling to apologize for her behavior the night before.

And well she should. He deserved an apology from her.

"Offer my nine o'clock coffee and hold on to him until line one is clear, would you, Brenda?"

He cleared his throat before he punched the correct button on his phone, and the stiffness in the muscles of his face yielded just enough to allow a small, satisfied grin.

"Zachary Jones here, Ms. Lathrop. Good morning."

2

JONES'S BUSINESSLIKE words echoed in Jenny's ear.

Hunched over her old-fashioned black telephone on its wobbly three-legged table, she came close to hanging up without saying a word. She scrunched up a handful of the long blue flannelette nightgown she wore and held on to it as if it were a security blanket.

She longed to hang up.

Except that he already knew it was her on the line, so she had to say something just to save face. Damn her impulsiveness! What the heck had she been thinking of, calling him first thing this morning?

Just what made her do it? It might have had something to do with the way his voice and presence invaded her dreams all night. She'd asked for one of his business cards from another aide at the clinic last night. The moment she got up this morning she'd headed for the phone as if she were hypnotized and had dialed the number.

Lord, she didn't even have a plan worked out!

"Good morning, Mr. Jones. I wanted to . . . Ah, I thought maybe I should . . . I wondered if maybe . . ." Disgusted, Jenny listened to herself stammer and stutter. She even felt herself blushing, for heaven's sake. She screwed her eyes shut, took a deep breath, and made a monumental effort at coherence. Inspiration struck at last.

"A problem came up last night with one of my clients at the Legal Clinic, and you'd already left. I felt it was important to ask your advice."

A moment of humming silence. Then: "Yes, of course. How can I help you?"

Was there more than a tinge of impatience in his tone now?

He sounded as if his nose was plugged. Well, it was probably swollen. His eyes would be puffed up, as well.

She tried to visualize him that way and failed, as she scrambled through the stack of papers from the night before and chose the notes she'd made about Veronica Glickman.

"Here it is." She outlined the scenario that Veronica had told her about yesterday, rattling off a half page of details from what she'd written down. She'd already more or less figured out what to do, but Zachary Jones wouldn't know that.

"Ms. Lathrop." The interruption was brisk and definite.

"Yes, Mr. Jones?"

"You did consider the possibility that this woman might be completely out to lunch? I mean, a bag lady, claiming to own valuable property in downtown Vancouver?"

"Mentally unstable, you mean? Veronica seemed quite rational to me," Jenny lied. "Just because she's older and poor and a bit ... eccentric, is no reason to suspect..." Jenny's increasing feeling of outrage showed in her voice. "I find that attitude discriminatory and unfair, Mr. Jones. All I wanted to know was how to go about helping her with this."

Now there was obvious exasperation in his voice. "Without knowing all the details, it's difficult to make suggestions. And I have someone waiting to see me. I suggest you begin by checking the title of the property at the registry office."

"She's coming back next Thursday. Maybe we could discuss it before the clinic opens?"

The words were out of her mouth before Jenny realized that her question was the real reason for her phone call.

She needed to know right now, this very minute, at ten minutes to nine on a Friday morning, whether or not Zachary Jones would be there next Thursday evening when Jenny arrived at the legal-aid clinic.

There was a long pause. Jenny found herself holding her breath. She knew that most of the volunteer lawyers attended only one clinic each semester and considered their duty done. She had no evidence that it would be different with him—especially after last night.

"That would seem the logical thing to do," he finally said reluctantly. "I'll be there a few minutes early and we can discuss this matter then. Goodbye, Ms. Lathrop."

"Wait—" Jenny's heart hammered with excitement at the thought of seeing him again. "I just wondered . . . Did you go and see a doctor last night, Mr. Jones? Was your nose broken?"

"Yes, I did, and no, it wasn't."

"I'm glad. That is, I mean I'm happy it wasn't broken."

His voice was a sarcastic growl. "So am I. Ecstatic. In fact, I consider it one of the high points of my life. Goodbye again, Ms. Lathrop."

Dial tone.

Boy, he was grumpy as a bear!

Jenny plopped the receiver back in the cradle and collapsed on the sagging sofa. The satisfied smile on her face refused to go away, and she felt exhilarated for any number of reasons.

She had no classes until one o'clock. For the first time in two years she wasn't exhausted from waitressing to earn tuition fees, and had time to perk a pot of coffee and sit here and drink it at her leisure.

And there was the sun.

A lot of mornings, the basement suite she rented was so dark Jenny was forced to turn on the overhead bulb to have enough light to make toast.

Today, rays of cheerful sunshine filtered in, illuminating the undeniably shabby furnishings and worn old burgundy area rugs her Scots landlord, Amos Carradine, had grudgingly donated to furnish the place.

Amos was so tight he squeaked, and Jenny had a hunch he'd scrounged the furnishings from the Salvation Army. Still, the suite was home to her, and most important of all, the rent was low enough that even she could afford it.

Jenny whistled while she scrambled eggs for breakfast.

Zachary was one weird name. Did his friends call him Zachy? She giggled, and popped two slices of bread into the toaster.

Thursday was still six days away. It seemed a long time, but Jenny was philosophical.

She was accustomed to having to wait. She'd waited until she was twenty-six to enter law school, and that had taken years of penny-pinching and part-time jobs.

She could wait six measly days to see Zachary Jones again. Couldn't she?

Not that there was any chance of a single thing happening between them. The idea was ludicrous. Jenny slapped margarine on her charred toast. As she munched on it, she tried to get a handle on Jones.

From all evidence, he was wealthy, arrogant, accustomed to having his own way—especially where women were concerned—as well as narrow-minded and bigoted when it came to social issues.

Yep. Zachary Jones epitomized everything Jenny abhorred in the male species. Look at that crack he'd made about poor Veronica!

He was no big deal, she assured herself, setting out her breakfast on the Formica-topped table she'd shoved under the window. She just wanted more time to figure out why she found him so intriguing, that was all.

THE FOLLOWING THURSDAY evening, Zach saw her right away.

True to his word, he'd arrived three quarters of an hour early, but Jenny Lathrop was still there before him.

She was completely absorbed in the documents she was reading. As he walked across the room toward her, her forefinger came up to shove her glasses higher on her nose in that vigorous, clumsy gesture he remembered.

Unexpectedly, all the irritation he'd harbored against her crumbled away and disappeared.

It was a wonder she hadn't put her eye out by now, doing that.

He hooked a chair with one hand and swung it into position so he could sit directly facing her. But then he changed his mind.

Yielding to impulse, he leaned on her desk with both hands and said in the roughest voice he could manufacture, "How come those meters out there won't take nickels and dimes, huh, lady?"

She jumped. Then she looked up at him and in slow motion, she grinned—that same mischievous grin that had so annoyed him the week before, and that emphasized the already upturned corners of her generous mouth.

She had kissable lips.

"Hi, Mr. Jones." She studied him with those astonishing blue eyes and gave a little nod of satisfaction.

"Your eyes look pretty good. The swelling's almost gone, and there's only a trace of purple and green at the inside corners. Your nose still looks fat, though."

He had to laugh.

"You sure know how to make a guy feel good, y'know that? What about the food stuck in my teeth? Aren't you going to mention that, as well?"

She gave him a look of mock innocence.

"Actually, I was going to let you find out for yourself. It's always a humbling experience, finding out you've got spinach in your smile."

Zach sat down, folding his arms across his chest and propping one leg on the other knee, and met her forthright gaze with his best businesslike expression.

"Okay, Ms. Lathrop. Enough frivolity. Let's get down to business, here."

She nodded, but she went on staring at him. "Are you going to be the consulting lawyer here for the rest of this term, or is this your last night?"

Her question was blunt, bordering on rude, and Zach hadn't a clue how to answer. He'd already come in for more than his share of flak from his partners about donating yet another valuable Thursday evening to the clinic. Specifically, they'd accused him of being into sadomasochistic behavior.

"Why do you want to know?" Being a lawyer made answering a question with a question easy.

She didn't even blink. "Because if you're going to stick around, I think you might as well call me Jenny. Ms. Lathrop makes me nervous."

"Fine with me . . . Jenny. But you'll have to get used to the formal mode of address with your clients, you know."

"Yeah, I do know, Zachary." He blinked, but she was scrabbling through a pile of loose papers and didn't notice. "I figure there's plenty of time for that—I'm just in my third year. Now, here are the notes I took when I talked with Veronica Glickman. And here are the details about that house. It's hers, all right. I checked at city hall. The way I see it . . ."

It didn't take five minutes to find out that the way she saw it was diametrically opposite to the way Zach would have viewed the matter. But these students were here to learn, and a large part of that learning, he reminded himself, was making decisions on their own. So he kept quiet and listened.

He reached for the notes she offered and let her run on, noticing her short, unpainted fingernails and the fact that she didn't wear any rings. He realized after a moment or two that she wore no jewelry at all. He'd always sort of figured women were born wearing at least a pair of small diamond studs in their ears. But Jenny had an inexpensive, utilitarian watch on her wrist, and that was it.

"What I did was get ahold of the health department. I got them to agree to back off until I can convince Social Services to send some volunteers over to the property and clean it up. I talked with a couple of social workers yesterday and . . ."

She rattled on and Zach nodded several times, paying more attention to the play of expression on her face than to her exact words.

"I mean, it seems logical to use common sense in a situation like this, don't you think?"

"I suppose that's as good a solution as any. But don't you see that the whole thing isn't a legal problem at all?" he asked.

"It's a human problem, isn't it?"

As Jenny continued to talk, her intensity reached out and enveloped him. Despite her efforts at containing her curly hair in a clumsy roll at the back of her neck, it tumbled loose around her face and bounced with each enthusiastic movement of her head.

She didn't have the typical pink complexion he might have expected with copper hair, though. Her skin was tanned golden brown, and was scattered with freckles that also appeared in the V-neck of her blue cotton blouse.

He found himself speculating as to whether her small, high breasts would be a startling white in comparison to her tan.

If she wore a bikini, there'd be that captivating tiny band of white skin again, intersected by the startling color of her hair— His body surged alarmingly.

"Zachary? Do you think so or not?"

She'd obviously been asking him something—several times, by the note of impatience now evident in her voice.

"I do think so. Yes, definitely." Zach tried to sound knowledgeable and positive about God only knew what, hoping his erection would subside by the time he had to stand.

"Good, I'll carry on the way I'm going, then." She gave him a wide smile. "Well, that's settled. I appreciate your coming early to discuss this." She looked down at her notes and added in a rush, "I really am sorry about you getting socked last week. I shouldn't have laughed. I tend to react that way when I'm off balance."

Zach studied the way her hair refused to part in a straight line on top of her head.

"No problem," he said in a soft tone.

"Well." She looked up and gave him a blinding smile. "It's going to be another busy evening, too. There must be a dozen people out there already."

Zach was suddenly aware of other voices; of subdued commotion in the reception area as the other law students took their places at the tables and desks. He felt oddly let down.

He stood and from across the room, Gloria waved to him. He raised a hand to her in a sort of salute and heard himself say to Jenny, "How about having dinner with me after the clinic's over tonight?"

The words were out, and he hadn't given one moment's thought to them before they spilled from his mouth.

Her smile changed, became uncertain, and then faded altogether. She shoved at her glasses with a forceful motion and frowned up at him.

"Why?"

"What do you mean, why?" Zach felt irritation flood through him. Couldn't she just refuse, instead of putting him through some dumb inquisition?

Besides, his ego was involved here. He couldn't remember the last time a woman had refused a dinner invitation. "A guy asks you to dinner, and all you can do is ask why?"

"I need to know, so I'm asking." Her expression was earnest and questioning. "Why do you want to? Have dinner with me?"

"I don't believe this. Let's see, because you need advice about applying your skills in areas that will most benefit your career in law? Because you need to learn some finesse when it comes to questions and answers?" Talk about fast on his feet. Imagine coming up with that high-sounding crap when all the time he was still wondering about her bikini line and the color of—

He gave her what he hoped was an ingenuous grin.

"Because I enjoy talking with you and want to get to know you better?"

"Bullshit."

She said it as if it were an ordinary, everyday word, and she went right on frowning at him.

Zach couldn't help himself. He started to laugh, because she was outrageous and absolutely right.

"Okay. I don't have the foggiest clue why I want to take you to dinner. You're difficult and argumentative but I like your hair. So, do you want to eat with me or not?"

She hesitated, and then nodded her head a couple of times. "That's pretty honest. All right, I guess I'll come."

ALTHOUGH THE CLIENTS that Jenny saw during the next several hours had the benefit of her full attention, not for one moment did she stop thinking about the date she'd made with Zachary Jones.

In typical female fashion—most *untypical* for her—she worried about her clothes. Her plain blue blouse and calf-length patterned cotton skirt was one of her favorite outfits because it was comfortable and easy to move in. Still, beside Zachary's elegant suit, it looked exactly what it was: an ensemble bought from the racks of a secondhand clothing store.

That didn't bother her in the least. After all, most of her clothing came from thrift shops. It was just that at home she had a sea-green rayon dress, acquired for eleven dollars at a garage sale. She'd have worn it tonight if she'd known. She'd hesitated about buying the darned thing because she didn't think she would have an occasion to wear it. And here was the perfect occasion. But, damn! The dress was crosstown in her closet.

It was a wasted opportunity, especially since there wouldn't be any second date with Zachary when she could wear the green dress. Jenny hated waste.

He'd said himself that he thought he was out of his mind, asking her out at all.

And she sensed in him all the characteristics she wanted *most* to avoid when she became a practicing lawyer.

But going out with him would be a learning experience, she told herself. She could learn a whole lot about the type of man she *should* avoid like the plague. Even negative learning experiences were valuable. Weren't they?

She dismissed the fact that he had the most disturbing effect on her heart rate whenever he was nearby.

HE TOOK HER to a restaurant hidden in a residential district of Kerrisdale—an old stone house with a wooden sign outside that simply read Philomene's.

They were met at the door by an older woman with shining silver hair, wearing a black silk dress and an air of absolute dignity. She greeted Zachary by his first name, gave Jenny a frosty smile, then led them into a tiny, completely private dining area and seated them at a round oak table set for two.

"Suzanne will be with you shortly, Zach. I'll send Antony in to take your order."

Soft piano music came from an adjoining room, and Jenny thought there surely must be other patrons around somewhere, but there was little evidence of them. She felt uncomfortable, as if she'd bungled into a private home, expecting dinner from people she didn't know.

Zachary was quite relaxed, however. He and Antony seemed to be the best of friends.

"Get much sailing in this summer?" he asked Zach.

"Not as much as I'd like. How about you?"

Antony launched into an account of a month spent surfing on the north coast of Hawaii before he got around to asking what they'd like to drink. Zach ordered a Scotch and water, but Jenny, wanting to keep her head clear, ordered a diet cola.

"Wouldn't you prefer a glass of wine?" Zach asked. But she shook her head.

"Not even with dinner?" He raised his eyebrows.

She glared at him and said no, and he shrugged, accepting her decision without any more argument, for which Jenny was grateful.

The menus were hand lettered and there were no prices marked. Jenny ordered a seafood linguine with a salad, and Zach wanted steak.

When at last the ordering was over with and they were alone again, Jenny began to relax a little. The atmosphere was tranquil, the piano soft and soothing, and she liked the private little alcove where they were seated.

"Well, Jenny Lathrop who doesn't drink wine." Zach's voice was lazy and just a little teasing. "Tell me about yourself."

Jenny sipped her cola and looked at him, tilting her head a bit in order to see through her glasses, which were on their inevitable journey down her nose.

"What do you want to know?"

He pursed his lips and considered that. "Oh, why you wanted to be a lawyer, for instance."

She studied him for a long moment. Was he being a trifle condescending?

She decided he needed to hear the truth.

"Mostly because my husband was killed in an accident six years ago."

Zach looked shocked. He'd been about to take a drink, but instead he set the glass back on the table, giving his full attention to Jenny. Her voice was quiet and controlled, matter-of-fact, as if she'd related her story many times before.

"He was working on a nonunion construction job, and a sheet of plate glass collapsed. Nick and three other guys were underneath it. It was negligence on the part of the company, but they wouldn't admit to fault."

She sipped her cola and shrugged before she went on. "We didn't have any kids, Nick and I, but all the other men did. The families received no compensation at all, because of bungled legal advice on our side and smart lawyers on theirs. The other wives had to take menial jobs to support their kids and pay off the legal expenses we all incurred in our fight for a settlement."

Her eyes were focused now on a picture on the wall behind him. "When the whole mess was over, I was good and mad. I took what money I had from a small insurance policy Nick left me and used it to go back to school. I thought it wouldn't hurt to find out what the law was like from the other side of the fence, and then maybe help other people with cases like mine. It was slow. It took me a year of upgrading to pass my LSAT, because I took most of my early education by correspondence, but I finally made it." She met his gaze now, her intense blue eyes watchful of his reaction.

Zach was looking at her in a different way than he had before. The laughter in his eyes had disappeared, and when he spoke, the teasing undertones were gone. He sounded apologetic, as well as embarrassed. There was something else, too.

Tenderness?

"God, I'm sorry, Jenny. About your husband. About . . . I didn't mean to pry. I never dreamed . . . I mean, you look far too young to have had all that happen to you."

Jenny suspected that in Zach's social circle, death and poverty weren't discussed over dinner.

Maybe they weren't discussed at all. Maybe he didn't want to hear anything heavy.

Well, in her social circles, no one ate in places like this, so how was she to know what was discussed?

So tonight could be a learning experience for both of them, she reflected with a tight enigmatic smile.

"I'm twenty-nine, in case you're wondering. I guess that's not middle-aged, but I don't feel very young at all. See, I was married to Nick when I was seventeen. We'd already been together six years when he died." She gave a little shrug and smiled.

"Back where I grew up, girls married young." She saw his eyebrows go up in silent questioning and added, "It was twenty miles outside a little coal-mining town called Fernie, in the Rocky Mountains of southern British Columbia. Hardly anyone's ever heard of it." As an afterthought, she added, "I grew up poor."

Just then, the waitress arrived with their food, and for a while, Jenny was far too busy eating the remarkable meal to talk much.

She was hungry, and the dinner was absolute perfection. Her linguine was smothered in scallops, shrimp, lobster and crab, as well as a marvelous sauce; and the dressing on the salad was an expert combination of gentle herbs and spices—unlike anything she'd had before. Every bite was heaven.

She noticed that Zach, however, was eating his own dinner with a lot less enthusiasm and appetite than she was.

Well, he probably took food like this for granted.

The fact was, he was watching her more than he was eating, but for some reason it didn't make her uneasy. She savored each mouthful, and when she swallowed the last bite of crab, she looked straight at him and grinned.

"Bet you're not used to feeding starving women."

"I'm not, but it's fun," was all he said.

He had already finished his meal, and she laid down her fork and folded her arms across her middle with a contented sigh, trying to ignore the sensual responses he stirred in her.

"That was fabulous."

"I'm glad you enjoyed it." Feeling that she scared Zach off with her bluntness, Jenny sighed, expecting they were about to exchange social niceties for the rest of the evening.

She was wrong.

"Jenny," he said next—and there was a seriousness in his voice that hadn't been there before—"I get the impression you don't quite approve of me. Why is that?"

He was turning the tables on her, being as uncomfortably direct as she had been, and Jenny respected him for it. But she wasn't about to reveal her innermost feelings to him, either.

"I don't know you. So how can I approve or disapprove?"

He gave her that long, level look. "Well, then, let's get on with it. Get to know me, why don't you?" His gaze was challenging. She found herself admiring the firm lines of his mouth, the deep cleft in his chin. And his long-fingered hands. There was an elegance about them—she could imagine them stroking a path from her neck down to her breasts....

She shivered. *Careful, Jenny.*

"Well, Mr. Zachary Jones," she began in a playful tone, "you're right, of course. Turnabout is fair play. So tell me about yourself. Why did you decide to be a lawyer?"

"Would you like to order dessert before we get into this? They have a great cheesecake here. I've had it before."

His politeness touched her. She was tempted, but her waistband already felt tight. "I'm full, darn it all. How about just coffee?"

The waitress brought two china cups of strong, hot coffee, along with a silver carafe for refills, and then they were alone again.

"Okay, now make with the answers," Jenny ordered, mock tough.

He settled back in his chair. "Well, unlike you, I can't say I remember deciding to be a lawyer. It was just taken for granted from the time I was a boy. There'd been four generations of lawyers in my family, and it was assumed I'd be the fifth."

"Wow, four generations! That's a heavy legacy to have to pack around. But wasn't there ever a time when you rebelled, when you wanted to be—oh, a rock star or a plumber when you were growing up?"

He laughed. "I did have one short lapse when I was about fifteen, when I wanted to be a pro football player. I got my nose broken, my knees severely damaged and three ribs smashed before I gave up on that and decided I'd rather live a bit longer. After that, it was law all the way."

"And you find it interesting?"

Zach hesitated for a long moment. She felt pleased, understanding that he was doing his honest best at giving her straight answers.

"I figure it's as good a way as any to spend your working hours," he finally said. "I specialize in litigation work, so it's not as exciting as criminal law."

Litigation: two parties, seeking legal counsel to attain a settlement of a dispute. Litigation was one of the most lucrative branches of the legal profession, partly because ninety-five percent of civil litigation actions settled out of court.

If there was one branch of the law Jenny liked least, it was litigation.

Zach was still talking. "Two friends and I set up our own office some years ago, and we're doing well. That's gratifying."

It might be, but Jenny couldn't detect much excitement in his voice.

"Did you find the work load in university overpowering?" she asked next. "Sometimes I feel as if a day ought to have twenty more hours."

He shook his head. "I didn't have to struggle to get by, but of course I had to study hard. Everyone does."

"But you didn't have to hold down a job while you were in school?"

Again he shook his head.

"Did you have any problems getting in? The law faculty seems to reject more applicants than it accepts."

"I was lucky. My dad and grandfather are both graduates. They put in a good word for me. Mind you, I still had to get good grades on the entrance requirements."

It was enough. He didn't have to detail the route he'd followed to gain admittance to the Faculty of Law. There were students like Zach in Jenny's classes— graduates of elite private schools whose entry into the law faculty was ensured by an old boys' network of fathers and grandfathers who'd been generous contributors to the university over the years. She had to swallow a lump of disappointment.

She'd been hoping he'd surprise her, and he hadn't.

It was his turn to question again.

"Was anyone in your family a lawyer, Jenny?"

"Are you kidding? My mom and dad were hippies. I grew up on a farming commune."

He didn't comment, but his expression once more revealed his surprise. Shock, maybe? She wasn't certain.

Jenny had been feeling wonderful up to this point. The relaxed atmosphere and good food had lulled her into forgetting about the chasm that divided her and Zachary Jones.

Their worlds were far apart.

After tonight, they'd go their separate ways.

But then, her natural optimism came to the rescue. If this was to be the only time they'd share, she'd better make the best of it. She felt an urgent need to know about him, to find out all she could in the few hours they had together.

Jenny didn't ask herself why she should need to know about Zachary Jones. She only knew the feeling was there, and that it was powerful.

She shoved her glasses higher on her nose and leaned her elbows on the thick linen tablecloth.

"Tell me, when's your birthday, Zach? When were you born?"

Might as well begin at the beginning.

3

"MY BIRTHDAY?"

For one crazy moment, he couldn't remember. Then he said, "June 30. I'm thirty-five years and three months old. Why? Are you interested in astrology?"

"I'm interested in understanding you better." She was serious and intense. "The sign you're born under tells me a great deal about what sort of person you are."

His disbelieving grin told her what he thought of that. "Okay, lay it on me. What am I like, Jenny?"

"You're a Cancer, the sign of the crab, and you don't reveal yourself easily, which is why you feel threatened at the thought of my knowing about you from your birth sign. Let's see now. You can be moody, but underneath you're a romantic. At the same time, you're practical and sensible." She gave him a wicked, teasing grin. "And you can get good and cranky now and then, too. Downright mean-tempered at times. In fact, you're meanest when you're afraid of losing something, aren't you? You're good at making money, though."

Zach did his best to hide his surprise. Her assessment of his personality disturbed him because it was pretty accurate and not at all flattering.

He'd been mean as an injured skunk when his last lady had said goodbye. Not because he was in love with her; just because she'd made the decision to leave him instead of the other way around.

But, he consoled himself, at least he had the ability to recognize his own worst traits. That had to count for something, didn't it?

It was disconcerting to have a person he barely knew zero in on his imperfections with such apparent ease.

This Jenny was full of surprises. She made conversational left turns like this without signaling, catching him unprepared. He found himself trying to second-guess what unlikely thing she'd say next.

"I guess you study your horoscope in the paper each morning for hints on how to conduct your day, Jenny?" He was goading her. He couldn't resist finding out whether her temper would flare.

She shook her head in serene denial. "Not on your life. I think it's wrong to let anyone else tell you what your life should be. You shouldn't ever give away your own power, even to the extent of relying on daily horoscopes. Don't you agree?"

He'd never given it a lot of thought, believing himself to be his own man in every instance.

"Sounds right to me. But if that's the case, why is my birthday important?"

She looked at him as if he were a little slow. "Surely you realize that astrology is an ancient and accurate science. I didn't mean you should discount the knowledge. Only that you should come to your own truths about it."

"And have you? Come to your own truths?" He realized how much he liked looking at her. Her face changed all the time, and her intense blue eyes seemed to draw him into their depths, even while her glasses acted like a barrier. It was her contradictory mix of passion and coolness that excited him.

At what point would her control disappear? That coolness transform into uncontrolled desire?

"How did you start relying on things like birthdays in the first place to find out what people were like?"

She studied him for a moment, as if considering whether or not to go on revealing herself the way she had been. Then she said, "My mother was a self-proclaimed white witch. She studied all the occult sciences. I absorbed a fair amount while I was growing up. A lot of the hippies were into that sort of thing long before the New-Age people came along."

Jenny Lathrop grew more complicated the longer he talked with her. More desirable, more challenging.

"And is she still a practicing witch? Your mother?"

"She's dead. She died two years before my husband was killed."

It was a matter-of-fact statement, not calling for any response from Zach. But again, it roused his compassion. Jenny's family seemed to have died off at a disturbing rate. Zach could only remember one person dying in his family since he was a child, and that was a great-aunt who must have been about ninety-seven.

"And what about your father?" He was almost afraid to ask.

Jenny shrugged. "He's somewhere in Mexico. He went there after Mom died. I get a card at Christmas, but he moves around a lot."

Zach couldn't imagine how that felt—not knowing where your father was. He thought of his own father, in his offices in downtown Vancouver every day as regular as a digital clock. His healthy, staid family all still lived in the house his grandfather had built on Marine Drive long before Zach was born. Even the house-keeper, Eva, had been with them since he was a baby.

Zach now had his own apartment, but it was taken for granted he'd eventually move home again. Preferably with a wife and family.

Family was important to the Jones clan.

"You're pretty much alone in the world, then, Jenny?"

She nodded, with a gesture of her shoulders that told without words that she was used to being alone and didn't mind it in the least. It made Zach want to draw her into his arms and keep her safe, free her from ever having to be bravely alone again.

And yet . . .

"In a way, I envy you that," he said in a quiet voice, and it was her turn to be surprised. She'd anticipated the usual social words of sympathy, but Zach added, "Being alone affords a kind of freedom I've never had the chance to experience."

Jenny liked him even more for that insight.

After that, they talked about certain professors they both knew, and disagreed with a vengeance about which they preferred. They went on to disagree about certain legal cases they'd both been following in the newspapers, and about the tactics of the lawyers involved.

They moved on to books they'd read. She liked spy thrillers and he preferred satire.

He played tennis. She never had.

She loved softball. He hadn't picked up a bat since he was thirteen.

They lost track of time, and it was long after their waitress had brought silver-wrapped mints and an astronomical bill on a crystal plate that they finally realized perhaps it was time to go.

ZACH SHUT OFF THE ENGINE of the powerful car in front of Jenny's place and turned toward her. She was tiny, almost fragile, beside him.

"I had a great evening, Jenny. How are you for time tomorrow? Want to meet me for lunch?"

She'd convinced herself that this single dinner was it as far as she and Zach were concerned. All during the drive home, she'd steeled herself to say goodbye with a light and nonchalant note in her voice, despite the knot of longing in her stomach that she couldn't seem to get rid of.

One evening with him wasn't enough.

Now she had to reassess everything and figure out—

Hell. She wanted to see him again—more than she was willing to admit. Her heart was hammering with delight, so why try and intellectualize it?

But she didn't want to seem too eager, either.

"I don't have classes in the afternoon," she confessed after a few seconds' silence. She was too conscious of his scent, warm and arousing and male, mingled with the expensive-car smell of leather upholstery.

"Funny, I seem to remember from my own student days how the profs all like a long weekend. How about meeting me at the corner of the Student Union Building and we'll go to the Faculty Club for a sandwich?"

She'd never been inside the hallowed doors of the Faculty Club.

If anyone asked, she'd probably say she considered it elitist to belong to a club that limited its membership to a chosen few.

Still, she was curious about the place.

And she wanted—needed—to spend more time with Zach.

Proceed with caution, flashed the warning sign in her brain.

But there was still so much to learn about him, she rationalized. It was really like knowing one's enemy, she reassured herself. Like taking a course in pesticides because you wanted to be an organic gardener.

Like flying straight at a flame if you were a moth.

"Meet you about one?"

She ignored the warning signals. "Fine. And Zach . . . thank you for my dinner tonight. It was delicious." She was trying to open the door when his hand closed on her shoulder and then cupped her chin, turning her toward him. His hands were warm, strong and gentle on her face, and a tremor of pure, overwhelming wanting skittered through her body.

His mouth came down on hers—warm lips, gentle pressure, hard and soft and coaxing. He moved his lips, sensually teasing hers with the tip of his tongue, entreating.

Her lips parted, and her tongue met his, warm and wet.

He kissed as if he was sure of himself. He kissed as if she was fragile, but irresistible. He kissed as if this was the only thing in the world he wanted to do at this moment.

As if he wanted more, as if he were holding himself back with the greatest difficulty.

When at last they drew apart, her glasses were steamy and crooked, and she had to straighten them before she could get out of the car. He tried to help her, gently and clumsily looping them at the wrong angle behind her ears.

"We'll have to be sure to take them off next time so they don't get broken. Shall I walk you to the door?" There was a gruffness in his voice that signaled desire.

She was breathing hard. She shook her head no. She wasn't certain she could deal with another, longer kiss, standing up in his arms, touching him with other parts of her body. He'd said "next time," hadn't he?

"Night, then, Jenny. See you tomorrow. Sweet dreams."

He waited until she was safely inside before he drove away.

He caught a glimpse of himself in the rearview mirror when he stopped for a light. He was grinning like a total idiot!

BEFORE NOON THE NEXT DAY, Jenny was having horrendous second thoughts about her date with Zach.

Her morning lecture was on mental health and the intricacies of admitting patients to institutions. By eleven-thirty, Jenny was certain she qualified as a candidate for just such an admission.

One minute, she couldn't wait to see him again. The next, she was certain she was making the biggest mistake of her entire life even associating with him.

What, exactly, was it about a simple little lunch date that was making her hands shake and her head ache? What was making her feel out of control and panicked about this whole thing?

She'd had dates since Nick died. She'd even had one significant relationship. Moderately significant. Well, it might have become significant if she'd been a little more enthusiastic and he'd been a little smarter than a stump.

Anyway, she wasn't a vulnerable recent widow, was she? Ripe to fall for the first sympathetic man who crossed her path?

So, what was the big deal here?

She trotted out all the things about Zach that irritated her—his Yuppie style of dressing, his privileged background, his attitude toward the law and its application, and, most disturbing of all, the gut feeling she had that he could easily have been one of the lawyers who outsmarted her and the other survivors in the negligence suit against the construction company. He dealt with cases like it all the time. His speciality, litigation law, was reason enough to keep her distance from Zach.

It was plain crazy to see him again. They were born to be in opposing camps. Why play immovable object to his irresistible force? She was bound to end up sorry.

But she couldn't, even for a moment, rid herself of the memory of that kiss last night. There was this overwhelming physical attraction between them, regardless of what her brain tried to tell her. And he was fun to talk to. And just thinking about his fingers on her skin made goose bumps—

"So, Ms. Lathrop, will you outline for the class the factors to be taken into account by a client considering informal admission to an institution, please?"

For the first time in two years of classes, she was caught without a single clue as to what the answer could be.

Damn Zachary Jones. He was turning her brain to jelly and making her crazy into the bargain. And there were exactly thirty-seven minutes left before she'd see him again.

HE WAS THERE, waiting for her. She saw him a full block away, lounging against a light standard, creating a flurry of head-turning among the female students hurrying past.

He waved long before she thought he'd noticed her. She hurried up and stood in front of him, a little out of breath, flushed and disheveled and ridiculously happy. For a long moment they stood and grinned at each other without saying a word, like a pair of simpletons.

Then he reached out with one finger and touched her on the chin for a second.

"Hiya, Jenny." The low, intimate timbre of his voice sent shivers down her body.

"Hello, Zach." She smiled at him.

As usual, he was impeccably dressed: pin-striped suit, pale pink shirt, blue-and-burgundy patterned tie.

"You look . . . great," she said.

Didn't the man own a pair of jeans?

"So do you."

Jenny beamed. She was wearing an outfit she was proud of because she felt it made her look professional.

She'd found the small-size men's tweed jacket at the Salvation Army clothing store and had it dry-cleaned. She'd also bought the dress shirt there. The shirt had needed several strong bleachings to make it white again, and last night she'd struggled with spray starch, ironing it. She'd made the almost-ankle-length navy tube skirt from a length of remnant fabric, and as long as she didn't sit in it for longer than three hours, it didn't bottom out too much. She wore tights and her only pair of classic black pumps: a find for eight dollars at the Army and Navy shoe sale.

"Busy morning?" she asked.

Zach shook her head. "A couple of clients. Nothing heavy. You?"

"Nope. Just lectures." And she'd ended up acting like the class dunce, but she wasn't going to tell Zach that.

"I'm starving, are you?"

She nodded with vigor, and he laughed and said, "Let's go find some food before you collapse, then." He took her hand and tucked it into the crook of his arm, making her feel tiny and protected.

They strolled the few blocks to the gray stone building that housed the Faculty Club. There was a sharp-eyed woman at a desk just inside the doors, obviously on the lookout for gate-crashers. She beamed at Zach.

"Good afternoon, Mr. Jones."

"Hi, Margie. Nice day, isn't it?"

Zach led Jenny to a set of wide, curving stairs leading down into an immense room. On the left was a dining area and on the right was a grouping of leather sofas and deep armchairs flanked by coffee tables.

Two men in tweeds and sweaters, and smoking pipes, sat reading. How could they, Jenny wondered, with that wall of windows and the magnificent panorama at their elbows?

"Oh, wow, look at that view!" she murmured, and Zach grinned down at her as if he'd arranged it personally for her pleasure.

The wide area was fronted with floor-to-ceiling windows.

The haughty maître d', whom Zach addressed as Alvin, led them through the busy dining area to a small round window table in a quiet alcove, seating Jenny with far more flourish and pomp than necessary.

She hardly noticed. She was busy studying the people around her, the food in front of them. She was absorbing the rarefied atmosphere of the university's privileged population—professors and senior executives in administration, who dined here in splendor with their guests.

"Would you like something to drink, Jenny?"

"Just water, thanks."

"I'll have a beer, one of the local varieties," Zach decided, and Jenny changed her mind about the water.

"That sounds good. I'll have one, too."

She'd crossed some kind of footbridge with him. She trusted him about certain things today.

Some of the awkwardness Jenny had felt the night before was gone. She didn't need to stay as much on guard anymore. She knew a little about the man sitting across from her now—inconsequential things like the fact that he sprinkled pepper with liberal abandon over most of what he ate, and that he took cream but no sugar in coffee, and that he had a way of looking at her that made her feel like the only woman in the room.

He had a laugh that came seldom but was contagious when it did. The pleasure his laughter gave her inspired her to say outrageous things.

She knew that he managed details like ordering and paying the bill with an ease Nick would never have attained in a lifetime. It made being with him easy.

She suspected that Zach treated all serving staff everywhere as valued friends and she couldn't fault him for that. She'd been out once or twice with pathetic men who thought it made them macho to be rude to waiters. Jenny had given each a tongue-lashing they wouldn't soon forget, and neither had asked her out again. She wouldn't have gone, anyway.

She couldn't acknowledge just yet that Zach had a profound effect on her. He simply made her feel charged with a special, joyful energy. He made her want to see more of him.

They walked out of the Faculty Club two hours and forty minutes later. Zach was holding Jenny's hand, and she was liking it a lot.

"I shouldn't have had that second beer. Now it's made my head go fuzzy," she admitted, squinting up through her glasses at the brilliance of the fall afternoon and wishing that the time had gone more slowly.

He watched and waited for her to shove her glasses back up on her nose, and she did, right on cue. He grinned with delight and said, "Hey, I know just the cure for fuzzy heads. Let's go for a walk in the rose gardens. Did you know that breathing in the perfume from the roses will clear the toxins from the beer out of your system?"

"I didn't know that."

"Neither did I, until I made it up a second ago."

"Maybe you should have been a fiction writer instead of a lawyer."

He smiled and then shrugged. "There's not all that much difference between the two sometimes, is there?"

A tiny bit of the shine dulled for her when he said that. There it was again—that cynical attitude of his toward the career she'd chosen and planned to pursue with integrity and honesty.

She withdrew her hand from his with deliberate intent. "I don't agree with you," she stated, and tilted her chin at an aggressive angle. "That attitude toward bending the truth where the law is concerned is exactly the thing that's most despicable among certain branches of the law."

He gave her an appraising glance and shook his head.

"Jenny, would you stop jumping to conclusions? I didn't mean that I believe dishonesty is acceptable. I meant that there's room for a lot of creativity in the practice of law, just as there is in writing novels."

"Oh." It was too nice a day to stay mad.

He stopped for an instant and slipped his suit jacket off, looping it over one shoulder with a careless hand. His shoulders were broad and smoothly muscled underneath the crisp pink shirt.

A bit shyly, she slipped her hand back into his free one. He gave her fingers a welcoming squeeze, and everything was fine again.

The rose gardens were only a few minutes' walk from the Faculty Club, and they wandered in silence for a while, drinking in the heady scent of roses in full bloom.

"I read an article a while ago on the effect smell has on people," Jenny remarked. "Certain generic scents have universal meaning, like the smell of bacon, for instance."

Zach was watching her with a bemused expression. Who else but Jenny would start talking about bacon in a rose garden, he wondered?

"Bacon?" he prompted.

"Yep. Even if you're a vegetarian, apparently the smell of bacon makes you feel wealthy," she explained.

"It goes back to thousands of years of tribal lifetimes, when fat represented wealth."

Zach laughed, and the sound gave her pleasure.

"Are you making this up?"

"Not on your life. This was a serious, scientific study on pheromones—smells that affect us at a subliminal level."

They'd wandered along a maze of pathways, and now roses surrounded them. A bench was nestled there, and he sat, spreading his jacket under them, then drawing Jenny down beside him, curving an arm around her shoulders so she was cuddled close against his side.

Not only subliminal smells affected people, she mused. Her heart was beating a rapid tattoo at being this close to Zach, and she was conscious of the scent of his freshly laundered shirt, the hint of clean male sweat, the faint, pleasant tinge of beer on his breath. He smelled good; he always smelled good.

She was aware, as well, of his heart pounding against his ribs just as hard as hers.

"Jenny, I can't be near you without wanting to kiss you."

His voice was deep and intimate-sounding; his mouth was close to her ear so that she could feel the words as much as hear them. If she turned her head the slightest bit, her burning cheek would rest on his chest. She could feel the warmth of his body enveloping her, pulsing around her.

Wordless, she turned her face up to his. With tender care, he unlooped the temples of her glasses from behind her ears and laid them on the bench at his side. He wrapped his arms around her and he kissed her, and

Jenny knew with certainty that this was right. Nothing that felt this good could be wrong. It was as simple as that.

The more he explored her lips and tongue with his own, the more of him she wanted. She moved her fingers up his neck and through his hair, learning its texture, memorizing the shape of his head and his jaw. She moved her palm down and put it over his heart, and she could feel the thundering madness in him, the same tempo that filled her with heat and pulsing desire.

"Jenny..."

His voice was choked and guttural.

When his lips moved to her throat and then down to the flushed skin above the opening in her shirt, she wanted nothing more than to throw her clothing and his into the bushes and sink with him to the bed of moss that covered the earth beneath their feet.

The heavy, sweet scent of roses surrounded them.

Roses were the most primitive of scents, and until now, she hadn't fully understood their power. Roses were an aphrodisiac. They had to be. She wouldn't be melting in Zach's arms this way unless they'd cast a potent spell on her.

Would she?

4

"MR. DAVID SOLOMEN is here to see you, Mr. Jones." Brenda's crisp voice came over the intercom a few minutes before ten o'clock the following Monday morning, snapping Zach out of a daydream about Jenny.

He hastily swung his legs down from the top of his desk and opened a file folder at random, scattering a few printed sheets around, making it look as if he'd been working instead of fantasizing for the past hour.

"Send him up, Brenda."

The weekend had been spent sailing—a two-day trip Zach had planned with a male friend weeks before—and on Friday evening, when he'd again dropped Jenny at her door, he'd felt a trifle relieved that the next two days were booked solid. Otherwise, he knew beyond a doubt that he'd have invited her out to breakfast Saturday, stretched that into lunch, extended it to dinner... and who knew where it would have ended?

Yet, provocative images of Jenny, naked in his arms, were strong enough to shove the other, more rational considerations right out of his brain.

He remembered the way her stockings had swished when she crossed those long, curvy legs....

Zach made a conscious effort to banish Jenny and get his brain onto business when a tap sounded on his office door.

"Come right in," he called. The door opened, and a tall, dark man came hesitantly in, his shyness apparent in his face when he returned Zach's welcoming smile.

Pay attention here, Jones. Forget legs and think law.

Zach got to his feet and extended his hand in greeting.

"Mr. Solomen, good morning. I'm Zach Jones. Have a seat. Can I pour you a coffee?"

Solomen refused. "I'm afraid I don't drink coffee," he said apologetically.

He took the comfortable leather armchair Zach indicated. He wore casual clothing, and nothing about him telegraphed a money message. In fact, he looked as if he just might have problems paying the firm's hefty fee, but appearances could be deceiving.

"Now, Mr. Solomen, tell me a bit about yourself and how I can help you," Zach suggested, settling himself in his chair with what he hoped was an air of attentive interest.

Solomen cleared his throat. "I'm a businessman. I own three Organic Produce Marts—one on Granville Island, one in North Vancouver, one in Richmond. All three are heavily mortgaged, but after a lot of struggling, they're finally starting to pay their own way. I just landed a long-term contract to supply two of the largest local vegetarian restaurants with organic fruits and vegetables, which will make a tremendous difference to my finances. I figured I was finally seeing daylight, financially, and believe me, it's been a long, hard climb. Then I received this."

Solomen opened the briefcase he'd brought, drawing out several sheets and putting them down on the desk in front of Zach.

"It seems I'm being sued by this organization called the Safefood Society, headed by a man named Paul Jensen."

Zach had heard of Jensen. His name was in the papers often in connection with environmental issues.

"They say here they've conducted tests, and certain of my products have unacceptable levels of pesticide residue. They've enclosed test results, and I have to admit they're right. I ran some tests myself and came up with similar results, not on all my stuff, but some." There was a note of disgust in Solomen's voice, as if he was appalled by the finding. "I know about this Safefood Society. It's part of a larger organization called Earthcare. Jensen's involved in that, as well. It's nonprofit, North America-wide, and it carries a lot of weight with the kind of people who buy my stuff. They publish a magazine every month, and their mailing list is extensive. They can bankrupt me without too much trouble."

Solomen sounded desperate and Zach understood why as the big man went on with his story.

"My fruit and produce are purchased almost exclusively through the Northwest Growers' Association because they have, in writing, guaranteed that their products are certified organic. I also buy from certain private farmers I know and trust, but there's not much doubt that the samples tested came from NGA."

Zach studied the papers. "So you feel the NGA are selling you produce under false pretenses?"

Solomen snorted. "Damned right, they are. And they're charging me and everybody else top prices for it, which we pay, confident that the food is what they claim it to be, and that they test the soil conditions regularly." His eyes narrowed and his jaw tightened. "What burns me up is that the real losers here are my customers. People who buy organic foods are willing to pay more, just as I have to, to ensure they're getting a totally natural product. It's going to ruin my credibility and probably my business as well, when this appears in *Earthcare* magazine. And damn it all, it's not my fault. I'm the little guy in this."

Like an echo he couldn't avoid, Zach remembered Jenny, over dinner that first night, telling him with bitter certitude that the little guys were always the losers when it came to legal negotiations. It had made him uncomfortable, because he couldn't help but recognize there was some truth in what she claimed.

Solomen was saying much the same thing now.

"See, they're a powerful group, the Growers' Association. They've got expensive grants and lots of backing from the government. Me, I'm just an independent businessman trying to make a living here."

Zach's mind was exploring the probable arguments, bouncing possibilities back and forth.

"Have you considered going to this Paul Jensen and telling him exactly what you've just told me? It sounds as if he ought to be breathing down their necks instead of yours."

Solomen nodded. "I've already tried that. He wouldn't listen. He's pretty fanatical, and I get the feeling he wants to use this whole thing as a way of stirring up people's natural concerns about the environment. I think he figures I'm a more visible target than the NGA would be."

Zach was inclined to think Solomen was right. He asked more questions, and Solomen answered them in his quiet, intelligent way.

"There's one more thing, Mr. Jones." Solomen met Zach's inquiring gaze with forthright directness. "I don't have the money to get into an expensive lawsuit. I know your firm is the best around, that's why I came here first. But unless you agree to taking my case on a contingency basis, I'll have to go elsewhere."

Contingency meant that the law firm would foot the bill for all the expenses incurred in preparing the case, with the understanding that if they won, they'd receive thirty percent of the settlement. If they lost, they were out costs, as well as expenses.

Zach liked Solomen, and the situation interested him, but he had to be careful here. Contingency was a risky business at best. He and his partners had an agreement that in questionable cases, all three partners decided whether or not to take the case. And his guess was that this one would be questionable indeed.

Taking on a government-backed organization like the NGA was a major undertaking, and environmental issues were high profile and touchy. The case could attract a huge amount of media attention, especially if Paul Jensen was indeed using it to stir up publicity, which could be either a very good thing for the firm or a very bad one.

Zach made an effort to explain to Solomen what the problems were—the problems he could see right off. And there were bound to be dozens more he hadn't even thought of yet. He kept his voice carefully neutral the way he'd trained himself to do.

"I sympathize with you, Mr. Solomen, but you have to be aware that this could be a difficult case to prove, and expensive to prepare for trial. We're up against proving beyond a doubt that the contaminated material came from NGA. We also have to prove that the contamination didn't happen after you received the produce. As I see it, the only way we could go in with an airtight case against your suppliers would be to have these Safefood people or someone like them standing by, testing your produce as it arrives, until a sizable amount of it is proved to be nonorganic. We call it 'continuity of the contaminated exhibits.' Is there a possibility they'd agree to doing that?"

Solomen grimaced and shook his head. "I know they wouldn't. Like I said, Jensen's more interested in finding a scapegoat than in justice being served, in my opinion."

"We're looking at a private investigator's services, then." Zach didn't say so, but the expense of that could be astronomical.

Zach asked several more questions, and then the interview was at an end. Solomen got to his feet, briefcase in hand.

"So, what do you think? Will your firm take my case?" There was undisguised anxiety in his voice. "Because if not, I've got to find somebody else, fast."

"I can't answer that until I've discussed this with my colleagues and looked into the whole thing a bit more. Can you give me a couple of days, Mr. Solomen? I'll be back to you by the middle of the week."

Solomen agreed, but there was a dejected slump to the man's shoulders as he left.

Zach watched him go, knowing the chances of his partners' agreeing to take on the Solomen case were almost nonexistent. Ordinarily, Zach would be in full agreement with them.

But this morning, he was uncomfortable with the inevitable refusal. For some reason he could hear Jenny's voice in his head, talking about people who were vegetarian, who used their limited food money to buy produce they believed was free from sprays, and who were being victimized here just as much as Solomen was.

What the hell was going on here, anyway? Was Jenny turning him into a bleeding-heart liberal? Next thing, he'd be lying down in front of bulldozers, for God's sake.

Get ahold of yourself, Jones.

For all her definite appeal, Jenny was woefully impractical in her approach to the practice of law.

He'd do well to remember that.

And while she was on his mind like this, he might just as well phone and ask her out tonight. He'd cancel his weekly squash game with Ken. As far as cardiovascular fitness went, he breathed a lot harder around Jenny than he did smashing a ball in a squash court, anyhow.

That way, if he knew he'd be seeing her later, maybe he could get some work done this afternoon.

"JENNY? Hi, it's Zach."

"Zachary Jones?"

"What other Zach do you know?"

"Well, there's Zachary Smith, and Zachary Brown, and . . ."

The hint of laughter in her voice brought a smile to his lips.

"Look, Jenny, I wondered if you'd like to have dinner with me tonight."

"Dinner? Again?" There was a note of incredulity in her voice.

"Whaddaya mean, again? We only had dinner together once before."

"Twice. Thursday, and then again on Friday."

"So, what do you do? Only eat dinner once a week? Besides, Friday doesn't count as dinner. We ate take-out pizza, remember?"

They'd driven down to the beach and eaten it watching the sunset over English Bay. He'd kissed her, and he remembered how her lips had felt—soft, tasting a little of mushrooms and cheese. It made his groin ache, remembering.

"I thought tonight we could maybe have seafood. Ever been to the Wharf?"

"I can't tonight, Zach. Tonight's my Aquafit. I need the exercise."

"Aquafit? What the hell's Aquafit?" He was aware of sounding annoyed. After all, he was willing to give up his weekly squash game, and here she was, turning him down over some dumb exercise program.

Her voice developed a trace of frost. "It's my weekly workout, and it's important to me. We do swimming and aerobics and stuff. It's the pauper's version of a health club."

"Oh, a health club. I belong to one, too."

"This one's not exactly like yours, I don't think. It's just a swimming pool. We do water aerobics."

"Well, what time are you done? I could come by and pick you up afterward. We could go and have a late dinner somewhere casual. Save the Wharf for another time. How about it? Doesn't all that exercise make you hungry?"

He waited for her answer, almost holding his breath. There was a long pause, and then, sounding as if the words were being pulled out of her with pliers, she said, "I guess that would be okay."

Zach relaxed. "Great. Fine. What time are you finished? What's the address?"

"It's the old YMCA building on Burrard. We're usually done about eight."

"See you then." He hung up before she could change her mind. Water aerobics, huh? She'd be in the pool. In a bathing suit. If he got there a little early, he could see for himself how much of her was tanned. He could study the shape of her thighs, the exact curvature of her hips and breasts... He locked his hands behind his head and tipped his chair back, giving in to fantasy.

"WATER TO CHEST LEVEL, class, knees bent, arm swings begin. Swing and one and swing and two . . ." The instructor's abrasive voice reverberated inside her head.

Norma had a voice that would have done credit to a drill sergeant. It bounced off the ceiling and walls and echoed from each of the corners. "We'll do our arm raises and leg pull-ups now. Double time, hup, hup."

Jenny rubbed at the lenses of her glasses with her fingers, trying to clear the steam off so she could see across to the clock high on the wall at the far end of the pool.

It looked like seven twenty-five. Another five minutes and she was heading for the locker room whether the class was finished or not. Norma hollered at people who quit early, but to heck with her. For several reasons, Jenny wanted to be safely dry and fully dressed before Zach arrived.

The first was that she'd feel more in control with her clothes on, and around Zachary Jones, she needed all the control she could muster. The second, more urgent consideration was that her old one-piece black tank suit had a hole in the back the size of a dime, right in the middle of her left buttock. Well, it might just have expanded to more like a quarter tonight...or even larger; without thinking, she sat on the rough concrete at the edge of the pool and slid in, and she'd felt it get much bigger.

It wouldn't have bothered her normally. She was here for exercise; what was a little hole in the bum of a swimming suit, anyway? Some of the women here wore suits so small there wasn't enough fabric to sprout a hole, for gosh sakes.

She just didn't want Zach to see it, that was all.

"Choose a partner, everyone." Just as she was about to climb out, Jenny found herself trapped into a group exercise, and for another seven minutes, she tossed a rubber ball to the stout woman on her left. The class was definitely running late tonight.

The instant the ballgame ended, Jenny hoisted herself out of the water. She was starting toward the women's locker room when, through her spotted glasses, she saw Zach sauntering toward her from the main entrance area.

Her heart sank. He saw her right away and smiled and waved, hurrying over to where she was standing, dripping helplessly all over the cement and cursing herself for leaving her towel in the locker room. She felt dreadfully exposed, even though he couldn't see the hole in the backside of her suit as long as she was facing him.

"Hi there, Jenny. I came a bit early. I didn't want to keep you waiting." He looked at her and grinned and shook his head. "Your glasses are all streaked. Can you even tell it's me?"

Before she could answer, he reached out and unhooked them gently from behind her ears. "Let me clean them off for you." He reached into a pocket and drew out a pristine white handkerchief, carefully polishing the lenses before he handed them back to her.

"Thanks. The chlorine or something makes them smear like that."

"Do you always wear your glasses in the water?"

She nodded. "I can't see the instructor without them. Or the other side of the pool, for that matter." She was calculating how she could reach the locker room without ever turning her back to him when Norma's unmistakable voice boomed from right behind her, making Jenny start.

"Lathrop, is your friend interested in joining our class?" Norma probably was a female power-lifter when she wasn't teaching Aquafit. She had muscles where most women didn't have places, and she was at least six feet tall. She wore black tights that came to just below her knees and she bulged in unlikely areas. Over the black Lycra tights she wore a skimpy red exercise suit. Out of the top spilled amazing segments of milky white breasts.

Zach smiled at her politely and shook his head. "Afraid, not. I just came by to get Jenny."

Norma moved in closer, ignoring Jenny and holding out a large hand toward Zach.

"I'm Norma Kaiser. I teach other classes besides this one. Maybe one of the others would suit you better."

"Zachary Jones. Actually, I belong to a health club already, and my time's limited, so . . ." He politely took Norma's hand and she gave it a hearty shake, holding on longer than necessary.

"Which club d'you belong to? I know most of the instructors around town."

Jenny edged away. This could work to her advantage. She could sort of sidle across to the locker room without Zach noticing, if Norma kept it up— But Zach reached out and took her hand before she'd gotten more than a single step away, restraining her. His eyes traveled provocatively down her wet body and back up again, and Jenny shivered.

"You getting cold, Jen? Sorry, Norma, we'll have to be going. Talk to you again."

He looped an arm around Jenny's bare shoulders and steered her toward the women's locker room.

"You'll get your jacket all wet," she warned.

"Forget the jacket. Just get me away from that amazon!" he whispered in her ear in such a desperate tone that Jenny giggled. Near the women's locker room he paused, and Jenny was several steps away when she remembered the hole in her suit.

He must have noticed by now. Instinctively, she put her hand back to cover the hole, but strong fingers caught her wrist and pulled it away. She felt herself blushing as she turned and met his amused green eyes.

"The things those designers won't think of to get a guy's attention," he said softly. He gave her a huge wink and a pat on the bottom, squarely on the bare area. "I'll be waiting in the hallway when you're done."

HE WAS THERE, lounging against the wall when she emerged some time later. He smiled at her.

She reached up and self-consciously smoothed back her soaking-wet hair. The women's dryers had been broken since the first time she came here.

She was wearing jeans, well-worn, with a tear in the right knee, and she had her funky boots on.

"All ready?" Zach straightened and reached for her bag, an old and battered one that had belonged to her husband.

He gave her another wide, welcoming smile and shifted her bag to one hand, reaching out for her with the other and taking her hand in his, swinging it between them as they made their way along the halls to the elevator.

"I was worried I'd missed you," he said. "I had to hide in the men's locker room there for a while. Your friend Norma caught up with me again."

"She's determined to get you into one of her classes."

He turned and looked down at her, and laughter was dancing in his eyes. "Actually, she offered me private sessions at the pool in her apartment building. And also invited me over for a drink while she works out the details of my fitness program."

"She did that?" Jenny was flabbergasted. "That—Why, that old . . . barracuda!" Jenny scowled.

Zach touched Jenny's arm. "Hey, it's okay. I told her my red-haired lady was jealous and held a black belt in karate."

"Damn right," Jenny agreed in a mock growl, but her heart pounded double time at his casual reference to her as his "lady."

It wasn't at all true, but it sounded so nice.

"Hungry?" He lifted an eyebrow at her, looking so well scrubbed and handsome she forgave him the small designer logo on the rear pocket of his jeans.

"Famished. I always am after Aquafit."

He teased her as they waited for the only elevator that didn't have an Out Of Order sign on it.

"Norma's not at all shy, I'll say that for her. I started thinking I was going to have to holler at you for help. You could have landed her one like you did that big ox at legal clinic."

Jenny snorted. "Some hope. She's bigger than both of us put together, and I haven't got my legal-advice manual. Forget it. You're on your own with Norma."

He gave a protracted groan and they got on the elevator, laughing like fools.

In the underground parking garage, half the overhead lights were out and a stale smell of urine and gas fumes hung in the air. The assortment of other cars were mostly economy models. Zach's shiny red sports car looked out of place and even ostentatious in this company. He unlocked it and handed Jenny in, stowing her beat-up sports bag in the trunk.

When he got in behind the wheel, he didn't immediately start the engine, however. Instead, he turned toward Jenny and studied her in the dim light, a curious expression on his face.

"How come," he asked slowly, "whenever I'm with you I have a great time? Even defending my honor with Norma?"

His words touched her, but she didn't want him to know that.

"Obviously," she said with a little shrug of her shoulders and a superior expression, "it's because I invite you to such swanky places."

"Now, why didn't I figure that out?" He took her chin gently in his fingers and held it steady as he leaned across and kissed her—a light, lingering kiss that left her trembling nonetheless.

He slid a caressing hand down her cheek and then, reluctantly, let her go and started the engine. "It's your night to make these exciting decisions, solicitor. Where do you suggest we eat?"

Jenny didn't hesitate. "One of my favorite places is close to here, it's a cafeteria-style place where they give you tons of food for hardly any money. Ever been to Fresco's?"

"Never. But if you recommend it, I'm sure it's great."

Was he teasing her? Too late, she remembered that economy wasn't exactly Zach's major concern in life. Well, maybe it was time he got to know about places like Fresco's.

He was gunning the little car out of the garage and up onto the street, whistling a tune under his breath.

"It's not very fancy, this place," she added belatedly, and he gave her a knowing smile.

"Somehow I never doubted that for an instant. Just as long as you promise me Norma won't pop out of the next booth wearing spangled tights and a G-string, I guarantee I'll love it."

"I promise. Well, I can't be absolutely certain about Norma, but I've never seen her there before. And they have a dress code, you have to wear a shirt and shoes."

"We'll just have to take our chances, then, won't we?" He reached out and took her fingers in his, raising them to his lips and feathering kisses across each knuckle, then grazing his teeth across her palm before he released her hand again to tend to his driving.

It wasn't the desire for food that made her stomach contract and her throat go dry.

5

"I CAN'T BELIEVE you've never been here before. Fresco's is a Vancouver landmark. You've been leading a deprived life!"

Jenny extracted one of the fries from the mountain on her plate and dipped it carefully in vinegar, then in catsup, and popped it into her mouth. They were seated in a booth. Besides fries, Jenny had a large bowl of soup and a toasted sandwich, plus rice pudding and a fat carrot muffin. She was starving.

"I've driven past lots of times. I just never had a reason to come in," Zach explained. "The food's plentiful, just like you said."

"It's open twenty-four hours, which makes it handy if you work till two or three in the morning and feel like eating something besides pizza."

"Have you done that? Worked till early morning, I mean?"

"Sure. Most of last year and the one before." Jenny chewed another fry and swallowed. "I worked at a pizza place to put myself through law school. I ate here sometimes. Pizzamania, where I worked, isn't far away. This year I won a scholarship, which made life a whole lot simpler."

Simpler in some ways, but far more complex in others, she mused. Zach was definitely a complication in her life—one she wasn't at all certain what to do about.

If only he weren't so damned attractive. She took a huge bite of her sandwich and realized he was watching her again, with that unfathomable look on his face.

She swallowed with difficulty. "It's hard to eat with you staring at me like that. Chewing isn't my best accomplishment," she complained. "What is it? Have I got catsup on my face?"

He shook his head. "I admire you, Jenny. You make me feel guilty for always having had things so easy," he said quietly. "I've never had to hold down two jobs or work half the night and then go to classes in the morning."

Guilt, or even admiration, wasn't exactly what she wanted him to feel at the moment, but she took advantage of it, anyway. "Good. That means that any day now, you'll give up this profitable litigation law and turn to something altruisic, right? You'll understand the error of your ways and turn your energies to helping your fellow man."

She was teasing, but he didn't smile right away. A thoughtful look passed over his features before he replied in a light tone, "Man cannot live by altruism alone, but sometimes it's tempting to give it a try." Then he told her about David Solomen and the predicament he was in.

"Of course, you're going to take the case?"

Zach studied the burger on his plate for a long moment. "I'd like to. But it depends on my partners' decision."

"I see." Jenny chewed reflectively, and her clear blue eyes said all the things Zach had known they would, about responsibility to his fellowman, about doing things for reasons other than money.

Her eyes made him uncomfortable, so he changed the subject.

"Speaking of altruism, how are you making out with that bag woman of yours—Glickman, wasn't that her name?"

Jenny shoved her glasses up and sat forward on the padded seat, excited about what she'd accomplished. "That's what I was working on today, actually. Remember her house was condemned by the city? Well, I got them to agree not to take action for a month on the house thing, I got the Downtown Residents' Association involved and they brought some pressure to bear on the city officials, which helped. And then today I got in touch with the Social Services Department. Veronica obviously needs their help, and they're going to send volunteers to clean the house up, inside and out. The next step is to get a cleaning service who'll go around on a regular basis and help Veronica keep order. I contacted several places today but it's hard to find the type she needs."

Zach had stopped eating and was staring at her again. This time, he looked more than a little horrified.

"I can't believe you got involved to this extent with a client, Jenny. You know all you're supposed to do is supply legal advice—not get mixed up with Social Services and the Downtown Residents' Association, for God's sake. To say nothing of cleaning companies."

She finished her sandwich and began to spoon up rice pudding, pretending nonchalance even though his words annoyed her. "I don't see why I shouldn't use whatever facilities are out there. That's the whole problem with the system. Nobody integrates the different services. And people like Veronica, who can't do it themselves, end up not getting the help they need."

His voice was quiet and she could tell he was deliberately being patient with her. "Jenny, there're social workers who are paid to do that. You're supposed to be a lawyer, remember?"

She shot him a dangerous look. She was close to losing her temper. "Yeah. Well, I'm a human being first, lawyer second. What do you expect me to do? Send her on her way with a list of suggestions she doesn't have the faintest idea what to do about?"

She could tell that's exactly what he thought she should do, all right. It made her blood boil. He didn't say anything for a moment, sipping his coffee in silence while the clatter of the busy restaurant went on around them.

Then he set his cup down and reached across the table, trapping her hand under his and holding on when she tried to pull away.

Having him touch her made it much harder to stay angry.

"Jenny, don't look at me as if I'm some kind of ax murderer, here." There was a pleading note in his voice she found hard to resist. "All I'm trying to get across is that people aren't always what they appear to be on the surface. Maybe this Glickman woman is genuinely a poor unfortunate soul. But even if she is, it's not up to you in your role as a lawyer to solve the world's problems."

"This has nothing to do with the entire world," she insisted, still annoyed with him but unable to resist the lure of his voice or the way he was stroking the back of her hand with his fingers. "It's a personal obligation I feel toward people like Veronica. A feeling that I'm capable and they're not. So somebody has to take care of them, right?"

How could he make her feel so . . . lustful, just by touching the back of her hand? Her mind was only half on Veronica Glickman. The other half was imagining him slowly taking off her clothes, conducting a full exploration of all her secret places.

"I admire your good intentions, but I don't want to see you get yourself in a jam." He put down the spoon he'd been toying with and rubbed a hand through his hair, still hanging on to her hand. "Damn it all, Jenny, how come every time we talk about work, we end up in an argument like this?"

She'd forgotten temporarily what they were arguing about. She was thinking that if his touch felt like this on her hand, for mercy's sake, what would it feel like if he stroked other, less public, areas of her body?

It was an image that had recurred more and more often the past few days. It made her insides turn hot and liquid, and she wondered—as she had with increasing regularity—when he'd get around to doing more than kissing her.

"I like to argue. That's why I like being a lawyer," she said distractedly, running her own thumb in a light caress across his palm and feeling a stab of pleasure when his eyes darkened and he swallowed hard.

ZACH WAS BURNING with desire. Ever since he'd seen her in that ridiculous bathing suit with the provocative hole in the bottom, he'd wanted nothing more than to find a horizontal surface and make wonderful use of it.

The problem was, for the first time in his adult life, he was trying to be a perfect gentleman. Each time he was with Jenny, he became more captivated by her, more intrigued—by her ideas, her opinions, her originality. Confrontational as she was, she made him think and react in a way he hadn't done before with a woman. He enjoyed being with her, and he wanted the friendship they had to continue—which meant that allowing sex to rear its lovely head would only complicate matters and perhaps wreck them altogether. He ought to know how that happened; he had a long history of bedding women first and talking to them later.

This time, he vowed, it was going to be different, even if it killed him—and at times, he wondered what the statistics were on death from sexual frustration. Especially, he pondered, at moments like this, when her blue eyes were sending him signals that set his body aflame.

His resolve weakened. She'd have to be unconscious not to know that she affected him physically. She must have felt the unmistakable hardness that signaled his need, every time he kissed her.

Maybe there was such a thing as being too much of a gentleman?

How the hell was he to know, when he'd never tried it before?

WHAT ON EARTH was holding him back, Jenny wondered? Reticence wasn't a problem she'd encountered with men; she'd always been the one saying no.

"Are you going to finish your food?" She jerked her chin at part of a burger and an almost-full cup of coffee on his tray.

It wasn't the first time since Nick's death that she'd ached for physical lovemaking. She was young, and she and Nick had loved passionately. But before, she'd been able to subjugate it with hard work, lots of exercise, and good doses of fantasy.

She knew that this time, none of those things were going to be enough.

She *wanted* Zach. The physical need weighed her down, making her body feel hot and heavy, making a pulse deep in her abdomen throb and ache.

"I've had enough to eat. How about you, Jenny?"

Food, yes, she longed to say. *Loving, no.*

"I'm full. Shall we go?"

My God, he was turning her into some kind of a sex junkie! She couldn't seem to keep her mind on what was going on. It was disturbing, because it was the first time that she'd fantasized like this about one particular, special man making love to her.

So what was the problem with him? She'd been out with him how many times—four now? And still he never got beyond heavy breathing and those kisses and touches that stirred every feminine response she owned.

He followed her out of the restaurant, courteously holding the door, taking her arm, settling her in the car. His manners were superb. And they irritated her beyond measure.

All she wanted him to do was act less like a gentleman and more like a hungry male animal.

"Want to take a drive around Stanley Park?" The car was poised at an intersection.

There wasn't a lousy thing they could do in this small sports car in Stanley Park. Didn't he realize that?

"I think I'd rather go home now."

She'd ask him in for a coffee. Wasn't that a euphemism any guy understood?

"Tired, Jenny?"

Lord, he was being thick. Was he going to dump her at the door and just drive away?

"Not bad. You?"

"Not at all. It's still quite early."

And surely, she pleaded silently, admiring his profile and casting surreptitious glances down at the outline of what she now knew were admirable thighs and awe-inspiring male equipment—surely, counselor, you can think of a great way for us to spend the next few hours? If you really use your imagination?

But she wasn't at all sure he was getting the message.

It came to her as they were threading their way through the narrow streets close to her apartment.

Zach just might have some kind of sexual dysfunction. She'd read that a lot of guys did these days. The professional in the article had said it had something to do with the changing roles of men and women and the new caution over choice of sexual partners.

Why, the poor guy! Her mind went over the list of problems in the article, wondering which particular one Zach suffered from.

Well, given an opportunity she was absolutely certain she could help him over it. After all, she was probably far more experienced than he was, given the fact that she'd been married and he never had. A warm, generous glow enveloped her, mixing pleasantly with the sensual yearning that had been growing inside her all evening.

The car purred to a stop, and before he could say a word about what a great time it had been and that he'd see her tomorrow, Jenny blurted out, "Care to come in for a coffee?"

Too late, she remembered the full cup of coffee he'd left behind only minutes before at the restaurant.

HIS HEART BEGAN to hammer when she asked.

He was almost at the limits of his endurance. The memory of her in that demure black tank suit with the provocative hole in the seat kept reappearing in his mind's eye; no matter how hard he tried, he couldn't subdue the aching need she roused in him. The silky black material had outlined her small, round breasts, clung to her tiny waist and emphasized the feminine cleft between her slender thighs.

But he'd made a decision about it, and he was a man who stuck to his decisions. Wasn't he?

If only she weren't so desirable.

She managed to be provocative without any of the trappings he was used to women wearing. She wore little makeup that he could detect, she smelled of soap instead of expensive perfume, her clothes were obviously designed for utility rather than seduction—and yet he wanted her more than he'd ever wanted anyone.

How the hell did that work, anyhow?

"Coffee sounds great."

He got her sports bag from the trunk and followed her around the side of the dark house to the steps leading down to her basement apartment, bending to help her when she fumbled and then dropped the door key on the cement; mindful of the warmth her body gave off, the smell of her hair, as she straightened and let him somehow find the keyhole and open her door in the darkness.

The basement was also pitch-black, even darker than outside.

"Wait here while I turn on the light. The switch is inside my door. Amos is an absolute fanatic about not leaving lights on. He comes down and unscrews the light bulb if I go out and forget to switch it off."

"Amos is your landlord?" Zach squinted around as the dim bulb in the entrance flicked on, revealing a cavernous area on one side, with an ancient furnace whose pipes twisted grotesquely along the ceiling.

"Amos Carradine, yes. He lives upstairs. He's a crotchety old Scot."

Cheap as dirt, too! Imagine sneaking around unscrewing light bulbs. Zach thought of Jenny coming home late at night to this absolute darkness, and it made him want to go up and throttle tightfisted old Amos.

Jenny unlocked a second door. "Come on in," she urged.

Zach had to duck his head under the low door frame, and even then his head seemed to barely clear the tiled ceiling. The living area was quite large, with a minuscule kitchen at one end and an open door at the other, obviously leading to a bedroom. Another door, closed, probably led to a bathroom.

It was generally homey and very clean. Jenny had used plants, homemade pillows and bright, colored throws to disguise the underlying shabbiness. Still, there was a large watermark down one wall that a travel poster of Mexico didn't quite cover, the ceiling tiles were badly stained, and it was obvious under the harsh overhead light that the whole place needed painting, and had for some time.

"Sit down. I'll put the water on for coffee. Or would you rather have perked? I've got a can of real coffee, if you'd prefer that?"

Her voice was unnaturally high and she seemed nervous, flitting here and there, patting cushions, turning on the only lamp in the room and switching off the overhead bulb so that shadows filled the corners. Her skin was flushed, her freckles stood out boldly. She shoved at her glasses several times with that one-fingered gesture he found so endearing.

"Instant's fine." Zach sat on the couch and found that the springs were gone. It sagged so much his rear ended up a scant four inches from the floor, which gave him a bit of a start.

Jenny noticed. "Sorry. That dumb couch! Amos rented me this place partially furnished and I swear he got the stuff from the dump. It made me sorry I hadn't kept the furniture Nick and I had. It was pretty junky, but it beat this by a country mile."

"You sold all your things when your husband died?"

Zach's curiosity about Jenny's husband overcame his natural tact. More and more, he found himself wondering at odd moments what the guy had been like.

Had Jenny loved him so much, no other man would compare? She'd been married six years. That was a long time.

What had their love life been like?

And how the hell could he feel jealous of somebody who'd been long dead?

She was in the kitchen, fussing with the small gas range and a kettle.

"Yeah, I did sell everything eventually. It took me a long time to figure out what I should do."

Zach loved the way gleams of light caught in her shiny, undisciplined mop of copper hair. He'd touched it, kissing her, and found it incredibly soft, but resilient, as if it held a life of its own.

He wondered what that hair would feel like, spread across his chest, gently tickling his stomach.... God. He almost groaned aloud at the instant response in his groin—the deep, aching need she roused in him.

Jenny left the kettle on the stove and came in and sat down on the sofa beside him, at the other end. She'd taken her shoes off, and now she tucked one bare foot under her bottom.

"We'd been living in a rented place out in Abbotsford. After Nick was killed I got to hating it, and it was too far from the university for me to even think of commuting, plus our car was old and not very reliable. So I had a massive garage sale, sold everything I could, and moved into the city. I was lucky to find this place. The rent's low and it's close to the campus."

Zach couldn't imagine anyone feeling grateful about living in a place like this. He thought of his own ultramodern apartment, the window wall with the panoramic view of the city, the comfortable, overstuffed furnishings—things his mother had labeled not quite suitable any longer for the house.

"It's certainly... cosy, all right," he managed to say.

The kettle began to boil, and Jenny jumped up again.

He watched her hips move as she walked away from him. She was slim, but there was a lovely flare to her hips all the same. The lines of her bikini underpants showed under her worn jeans, and he wished he'd told her he didn't want any coffee. He was hot enough without it.

But she was back in a moment, with two steaming mugs balanced on a painted tray that advertised a local beer company.

"Cream, no sugar, right?"

"Right. Thanks."

This time, she sat down more in the middle of the couch, closer to him. She placed the tray and her own mug on a small table beside the couch and pulled her foot up again, this time letting her knee rest against his thigh.

Zach liked that a lot. In fact, being a gentleman had lost every bit of its appeal in the last few moments. He figured he'd take two sips of the coffee, abandon it on the floor, and then reach over and—

But she was up again, turning the knob on a small transistor radio, tuning in a love ballad from a local FM station.

And this time, she managed to sit back down right beside him, twisted a little toward him. Her small palm seemed to come to rest on his thigh quite by accident, and she started stroking back and forth in an absent-minded gesture that had Zach nearly frantic in two seconds.

In the dim light her blue eyes were wide and unnaturally shiny as she smiled at him.

Then she cleared her throat, as if something were stuck there, and, in a voice barely above a whisper, she said, "It's awfully warm in here, isn't it? Would you like to take your jacket off, Zach?"

It *was* warm. In fact, he felt as if he might be on fire. But something was starting to dawn on him, and if he was right, he wouldn't ruin it for the world. Zach couldn't really think a whole lot, but it had begun to dawn on him that Jenny might just have a game plan here. Something was happening, and whatever it was, he didn't feel any need to analyze it.

She reached over a little hesitantly and begun easing the garment off his shoulders, resting one hand innocently on his chest for a moment while she slipped the jacket down his arms, following its slow journey with her hands in a manner that could only be described as incendiary.

God, he was right. This delicious, funny, wonderful girl was trying to seduce him. He'd had dreams about this, but he'd never for one moment thought they might come true.

"There now," she said soothingly, tossing his coat rather carelessly onto the couch behind her. "You'll be much more comfortable this way, don't you think? Why don't you slip your shoes off, as well?"

He slid his feet out of his loafers.

They were sitting very close now, and Jenny's hand was still on his chest, running back and forth in the same provocative way it had done on his thigh. He could feel his nipples tense each time her warm palm rubbed over them through the T-shirt. There was no disguising the fact that his jeans were becoming more and more uncomfortably tight.

"I'll just pull this out—" she was tugging on his T-shirt now, pulling it out of the waistband of his jeans with some difficulty.

Zach, mesmerized by what he now knew was about to become a full-scale seduction, did all he could to help without startling her, praying that she'd go on . . . and on. . . .

"—and slip my hands up under here.... Mmm, your skin feels so good, Zach."

Her breath caught in her throat and he could feel her shudder. She'd moved so that her breasts were pressing against his arm, rubbing against him the way a cat would rub, back and forth, in slow, sinuous movements. He could feel how hard her nipples were through the thin cotton.

His breathing was erratic. Nothing had ever aroused him more than this sweet, half-wanton, half-shy approach she was taking, and the last thing he wanted to do was to stop her. He exerted an iron will over his raging need and sat passively, letting her do whatever she wished as disjointed thoughts raced through his brain.

The fact was, he couldn't take much more of this. He'd been about thirteen the last time he'd climaxed with his pants on, but he was in grave danger right now of having it happen again.

Would she suddenly pull away if he turned the way he longed to and gathered her into his arms?

Carefully, he slid an arm around her, snuggling her even closer to him.

She moaned, and with clumsy precision, reached up and grasped his hair in her fingers, drawing his head down to hers, meeting his impatient lips with an eager, wet, openmouthed kiss that shattered the last shred of his composure.

His arms went around her and he expertly positioned their bodies so that she was against him. He took control of the kiss, savagely using lips and tongue to communicate to her his intense need.

But her glasses were in the way, so with one trembling hand he unhooked them from her ears. She didn't seem to care about the glasses or their fate. She was fully engaged in kissing him, nibbling all around his mouth, moaning moist, wordless promises in the vicinity of his ear, blindly pressing sweet, swollen lips fully on his and using her tongue in intriguing, somewhat clumsy stabbing motions.

He reached an arm out and dropped the glasses on what he hoped was the rug.

She used the moment to wriggle until she was lying fully on top of him, and the way her hips moved against his erection sent a fresh warning to his muddled brain. She was nibbling her way across his chest now, her hot, wet mouth accurately finding his erect male nipples through the T-shirt and gently tugging on them.

He fought for control. He had to slow this down, he had to get their clothes off, he needed to get them on some sort of a flat surface—the sofa slouched beneath them like a hammock.

"Jenny." His voice was rough and urgent, desperate. "Jenny, your bedroom . . ."

He interpreted the muffled sound she made against his chest as approval. He tried to get up with her in his arms, but the sagging sofa made it impossible, so he untangled her body for an instant, praying the spell would hold.

When he was on his feet, he reached down and scooped her up.

She was light and almost boneless in his embrace. It gave him the most incredible sense of power to hold her small frame in his arms. She put her arms trustingly around his neck, and went on kissing his throat and then his chin as he hurried them to the bedroom.

There was just enough light from the other room to make out the shape of the bed. He laid her gently on it, and in two practiced, easy motions, he stripped off his jeans, socks, T-shirt and briefs. There was a necessary item in his wallet, in the back pocket of his jeans, and he extracted it before he dropped the whole mess of clothing to the floor and sank down beside her.

JENNY COULDN'T HELP but feel a trifle smug about the success of her plan to entice Zach—when her brain let her think at all.

Mostly, she was just feeling—a wild and raging desire, a sense of exultation, along with intense, throbbing anticipation.

She waited impatiently while he took off his clothes. To save time, she sat up enough to tug off her own T-shirt, and she was struggling with the button on her jeans when strong hands covered hers.

"Let me." His whisper was smoky with an echo of her own passionate need.

Deftly, he undid her jeans and eased them down her hips, kneeling on the bed beside her, letting his hands trail along the naked skin as it was uncovered.

"Jenny. Lovely Jenny, you're so tiny, so soft...."

Only her bra and bikini panties remained. He ran a finger under the elastic at her leg, tantalizing her, finding a warm, moist spot that surged toward his finger when he touched it, tempting them both with the promise of release.

Jenny opened her eyes, wanting to see him, wanting to know what the hidden parts of his body looked like.

She couldn't get a clear picture without her glasses, but even in the dimly lit blur, she could tell that Zach was as magnificently constructed as she thought he would be. She wanted to reach out and take him intimately in her hand, but suddenly a wave of shyness came over her.

He was on the bed beside her. The plywood she'd put under the mattress made the surface extra firm, but a niggling concern came and went in her mind as the bed moved with his weight.

Would the block of wood she'd used to prop up the corner where the leg had fallen off hold up to their lovemaking?

But Zach was kissing her again, undoing the front catch on her wispy bra, exploring her breasts with tender fingers, letting his mouth trail cleverly down her neck, down . . .

"Jenny, you're so perfect, you fit exactly in my palm. . . ."

A gasp caught in her throat as his hot mouth closed around her right nipple. His lips and tongue knew exactly what to do, and she writhed as the electric sensations he created inside her rippled down to her abdomen and caused bursts of fiery desire to explode between her thighs.

"Jenny, touch me. Put this on for me . . . for us. . . ."

He slid a tiny packet into her hand, and she forgot to be shy.

She closed one hand inquiringly over his substantial arousal. With the other, she gently rolled the protection into place.

His fingers traveled down to the damp spot where fire was throbbing between her legs. Beyond control, beyond reason, she surged against his touch.

"Please, Zach. Oh, please, now . . ."

The feel of him in her hand combined with the knowing touch of his fingers brought her to the brink of climax, and in another instant, he'd slid inside her, infinitely gentle but pressing deeper and still deeper until she was filled with his heat and size and power.

He paused, murmuring love words to her, telling her how perfect she was. Then he moved, long and slow, and she was lost.

She stiffened and called his name while speech was still possible. She heard him make a deep, guttural sound in his throat, and he drove himself into her, arching his body with hers.

Their voices joined in a wild incantation, and the echo was still in the room when the block of wood gave way and the foot of the bed collapsed beneath them with an earsplitting crash.

6

"WHAT THE BLOODY HELL . . . !"

Zach held on to her, protecting her as well as he could, as they slid abruptly to the floor. They ended in a tangled heap of arms and legs, with Jenny sprawled on top of him, and it took several confused moments to sort themselves out and sit up.

Jarred from the heights of rapture to the depths of absurdity, Jenny began to giggle. They were sitting on a puddle of clothing, her underwear and his jeans tangled together in disarray. Pillows and sheets and blankets were flung all around them on the worn rug, with the rough sheet of plywood she'd inserted under the thin mattress in plain view.

"God almighty, we've gone and broken your damned bed!" Zach sounded so horrified and disgusted, Jenny couldn't stop laughing to explain. At last she got control of herself.

"Zach, I'm . . . I'm sorry. It's not us. This bed is really just a set of springs on iron legs. The springs were saggy and one of the legs came off shortly after I moved in. So I got this piece of plywood for under the mattress and I propped the broken leg up on that piece of wood. I'm normally a quiet sleeper and I don't weigh much, so it's never been a problem till now. It did cross my mind when we first . . . But things were so nice, and I just hoped . . . You're not mad, are you?"

She squinted at him in the semidarkness, trying to decipher the expression on his face.

He was silent for a long moment, and her heart sank. He was probably used to sipping wine on silk sheets after making love.

He reached out and ran a gentle finger down her cheek. "No, sweetheart, I'm not angry."

Sweetheart. He'd called her *sweetheart*.

"I'm sort of . . . flabbergasted," he went on in a deep rumble. "Quite apart from landing on the floor, what happened between us was pretty incredible." He cradled her head between his palms and rested his forehead on hers, then ran his fingers through her hair and caressed her ears, her neck, with sensitive fingers.

"Jenny, whether you know it or not, you're unique. I've never met anyone like you in my entire life."

She was very still, and she closed her eyes a moment to consider his words.

"Is...is that a good thing, Zach?" Her voice was soft and hesitant. "I mean, a person could take that different ways."

"It's the best," he said fervently. "Tonight is one of the best things that ever happened to me. Apart from the stupid bed, of course."

Right then, sitting on the floor naked amid the wreckage, she realized that she was in the process of making a fatal error. She was falling in love with Zachary Jones.

It was a frightening realization, and there didn't seem to be a lot she could do about it. It had crept up on her, and somewhere in her subconscious she'd known it was happening all along.

"Jenny?" His voice penetrated her reverie. The room was chilly and he was wrapping a blanket around her shoulders. His tone was uncertain. "Jenny, do you...uhh, is there some reason that you...well, that you'd rather take the initiative in lovemaking?"

"Take the—" For an instant, she couldn't figure out what he was talking about. Her seduction plan had been so successful, she'd forgotten about it halfway through. She snuggled into the soft blanket and shook her head. "Oh. That. No, of course not. I just figured because...well, you seemed kind of...reticent...and I thought you maybe had some kind of problem. I read this article that said a lot of men do, so . . ."

There was silence again, and then she could hear the astonishment and a hint of laughter in his voice when he said, "You thought I had a problem? A sexual problem, like impotence, or—?"

Her defense came quickly. "Well, you never went beyond kissing. What was I supposed to think, for goodness' sake?"

There was laughter in his voice. "Jenny, for the first time in my entire life, I was trying my damnedest to be a gentleman."

That possibility had never occurred to her.

"Ohh," she said after a while, relieved that there wasn't enough light for him to see the flush creeping up her face.

"It was sweet of you to want to help me, though."

He got up from the floor and started rearranging her bedroom. He tossed their clothing onto the chair and gave the mattress a yank. It came off the lopsided frame altogether and landed on the floor. He propped the frame on end against the wall, and now there was room for the mattress on the rug. Her pink fitted sheet was still intact except for one corner, and he tucked that under and then grabbed the rest of the bedding and pillows, making them into a clumsy, tumbled nest on top of the mattress.

She was still sitting on the floor, bundled into her blanket. He reached over and drew her with him onto the mattress, snuggling them both into the cocoon he'd made.

"At least this way the damned thing can't fall anywhere," he muttered, loosening her blanket.

Her breath caught when her warm body encountered his cool nakedness. He enclosed her in his arms, wrapping himself around her. His hands skimmed her rib cage, cupped her breasts and slid with tantalizing slowness down to her thighs. She could feel his hardness pressing against her. She adored the texture of his chest hair tickling her breasts. It was intoxicating to be able to run her hands anywhere she chose, touching, learning the feel of his skin, stroking the most intimate places on his body, here . . . and here . . . and there. . . .

He made a sound deep in his throat—of pleasure and impatience.

"Now, my little therapist. About that sexual problem of mine . . ."

HOURS LATER, Jenny had her blue flannel nightgown and her glasses on, and she was cooking them eggs and toast. It was long after midnight.

Zach was seated at her little table, making it look ridiculously small and rickety. His feet were bare, his legs sprawled out in front of him. He'd pulled on his jeans and T-shirt, but his hair was all tousled, and his eyes had the same half-closed, satisfied look she'd seen in her own eyes in the bathroom mirror.

He looked good. She kept stealing glances at him as she buttered the toast and found catsup and strawberry jam for the table. It seemed both strange and somehow right, being with him like this.

"Thanks, Jenny." He eyed the plate of eggs, fried tomatoes and toast appreciatively and picked up his fork when she sat down across from him. "I didn't realize you could cook."

"This isn't exactly a four-course meal, but yeah, I do like cooking. The way I grew up, everyone had to take their turn in the kitchen, preparing food for others. It was a challenge. We mostly used the stuff we grew ourselves. How about you? You like cooking?"

Zach was attacking his eggs eagerly. He shook his head, smearing jam on a piece of toast. "I can get cereal into a bowl, and I open cans without too much trouble. But beyond that, I'm lost. We've always had a housekeeper, Eva, at home. She's a marvelous cook and hates anyone messing around in her kitchen. She used to make me anything I wanted. So I just never learned."

Of all things, servants! She should have guessed it. Once again, the differences between her and Zach were glaringly obvious.

She kept her tone light. "You really had an underprivileged childhood, you poor man. We all had to help with the huge garden in the summer. I was always in the kitchen, peeling vegetables or tearing lettuce for salads. We made tons of salads. Most of the commune was vegetarian."

He gave her a curious look. "You're not now, though? Vegetarian?"

She shook her head. "Not strictly, no. I just don't eat red meat, and I buy organic produce whenever I can."

"Like what Solomen sells. He says it's more expensive. Is it worth it?"

"It does cost a little more, but it's worth it. No pesticides or anything. Amos lets me plant a few zucchini, carrots and lettuce in the backyard here. I share the crop with him. When I'm rich, I'm going to have enough land to grow all my own vegetables."

He smiled at her, feeling both tender and amused.

"You're just a country kid at heart, Jenny."

"Darned right," she agreed.

IN HIS OFFICE the next morning, Zach kept hearing Jenny's voice, talking about gardening. He was having disturbing flashbacks of other segments of the evening, as well, but it was the damned organic vegetables that truly haunted him.

He should have known Jenny would be one of the people who spent what little money they had on organic produce—which was anything but organic, thanks to suppliers like Northwest Growers.

Over morning coffee, Ken and his other partner, Derek, had turned thumbs down on the Solomen case—just as he'd feared they would—using all the practical, hardheaded arguments he'd thought of himself.

Well. He'd better phone Solomen and give him the news. There was a lawyer Zach recommended at times like this—a man he'd graduated with who always seemed eager to get into dubious cases; a passionate, fiery sort of guy who wouldn't balk at contingency.

Zach picked up the phone, began to dial Solomen's number, then slammed down the receiver halfway through.

Damn it all. He wanted this case himself, and he was going to take it.

No, he corrected. The firm was going to take it.

His partners owed him a couple of favors when you came right down to it. There was that fiasco with Ken's uncle a couple years ago, a drunk driving charge. Zach had gone to court with the older man himself as a personal favor to Ken—and gotten a tongue-lashing from the judge, as well as losing the case. Which was a blessing, considering the guy's driving record.

And that breach-of-promise thing Derek had gotten himself involved in with that real-estate woman. It had taken all three of them to get him off the hook on that one.

He pushed the intercom. "Brenda, are Ken and Derek with clients right now?"

"No, Mr. Jones. Mr. Meredith is on the phone, and Mr. Hanover is in the washroom."

"Tell them both to meet me in Ken's office in five minutes, would you?"

Zach had to forcefully remind his partners of their past follies and endure their accusations about going soft in his old age. Half an hour later, though, he was able to call David Solomen and tell him Meredith, Hanover and Jones would be happy to take his case, on contingency.

It was an exaggeration, of course. Jones was happy to take the case. Meredith and Hanover were decidedly unhappy about it.

"This whole thing could blow up in your face, Zach," Ken warned. "It's going to cost a bundle, and even if you win, the settlement isn't going to be that great, anyway."

Zach knew all that. But, for the first time in a long while, he was filled with excitement about a case he was handling. It meant something to him, quite apart from dollars and cents.

THE OTHER ISSUE Zach had decided to deal with was a personal matter. He'd spent the hours after he left Jenny last night figuring out a plan and drafting a written agreement.

He left the office at two-thirty. Jenny had told him she had classes all afternoon, so he knew the coast was clear.

He drove to her neighborhood and parked in front of Amos Carradine's house, marched up the walk, briefcase in hand, and rang the bell.

Carradine was tall—the same height as Zach—and he looked to be in his sixties. He was white-haired, as thin as a cadaver, and the deep, disapproving lines on his face looked as if smiling might do him permanent damage. He opened the front door after Zach had rung three times.

"What d'ya want?"

"Mr. Carradine? My name is Zachary Jones. I'm a friend of Jenny Lathrop. I'd like a word with you."

The piercing bleached-blue eyes flicked from Zach's face to the red sports car parked at the curb, and he made a contemptuous noise in his throat.

"Friend, ya say? Friend, hah! Ye're the one was down there half the night. Don't think I don't know what's goin' on. No morals. That's what's wrong with you young people today."

Zach ignored the attack for the time being, even though it made his blood boil. There were more important things to settle first.

"Mr. Carradine, I'm a lawyer. I'm here in a professional capacity and I'm afraid I have a few unpleasant truths to discuss with you. Do you want to conduct this conversation out here—" Zach glanced pointedly at the avidly interested neighbor raking up leaves on her lawn "—or do you think I could step inside for a moment?"

Carradine's frown became ferocious, but he grudgingly moved back and allowed Zach just inside the door, keeping him standing in a dingy hallway.

"Mr. Carradine, I understand the suite you rent downstairs is not registered at city hall, and Jenny tells me she pays you her rent in cash."

It was an educated guess. Jenny had told him no such thing, but Carradine's suddenly wary expression confirmed Zach's suspicions.

"And what business is that of yours?" The growling voice was low and menacing, and the cool smile Zach gave the unpleasant man in return was a lethal warning.

"I'm making it my business. You understand you're facing a heavy fine if anyone complains," Zach went on smoothly. "And then there's the matter of income tax, as well. It's a serious thing, not claiming income, isn't it? Now, Mr. Carradine, I've seen the premises downstairs and I know what Jenny's paying you for them."

He'd asked her, and although the rent was low, it was far more than the place was worth, in his opinion. He told Carradine so. "Quite frankly, she could easily find something much better for the same money, but for some obscure reason, she actually likes living in your basement suite. So that means you're going to have to make some changes down there, doesn't it? Because that place isn't fit to rent out at all, the way it is. It wouldn't be hard to have it condemned."

"You dare come in here and tell me what I'm going to do? You . . . you . . . I ought to . . . Get off my property!"

Carradine had been growing more and more red-faced, and the final words were nothing short of a bellow, accompanied by a fist shaken in Zach's face.

Zach suspected Amos had intimidated quite a few people in his time. He certainly had the lungs for it. Zach kept his voice reasonable, although the urge to physically attack the cranky old miser was almost overwhelming.

"I wouldn't consider anything hasty if I were you, Carradine. As I told you, I'm a friend of Jenny's. A very good friend. And from what I saw down in that dungeon you call a suite, she needs a friend badly in her dealings with you. Now here's what you're going to do. Unless, of course, you'd rather I made a call to city hall. And the income-tax department. And maybe the health officials."

Zach outlined his conditions and opened his briefcase, producing the agreement he'd drawn up. "This stipulates that you won't raise Jenny's rent for the next year. In return, I'll pay for the paint and supply a new sofa and bed—but I want a good job done, repairs made where they're needed. You hire workmen. No slapping cheap paint over the whole mess. See to it everything's done right, or you'll answer to me."

The elderly man was purple in the face, but he had little choice except to sign the paper. Since Zach was paying for some of it, Carradine wouldn't be out of pocket a great amount—Zach didn't really know how well-off the old man was, when it came right down to it.

"There's no need for Jenny to know about this meeting, or the agreement, is there, Mr. Carradine? Let's do your reputation some good and let her think the whole thing was your idea." Zach handed Carradine a copy of the agreement. "Oh, and two more things." Zach abandoned his reasonable tone of voice, allowing his anger and disgust to show.

"The first is that damned light in the hallway. From now on, it stays on. She could break her neck down there in the dark. The second thing is, you don't seem to understand that a tenant like Jenny has a right to privacy. What goes on down in her suite is her business, and if I hear even a whisper of you saying things to her like the things you said to me when I arrived today, I won't just be phoning city hall and reporting you, Carradine. I'll be over here discussing it man to man. You understand what I'm saying?"

Carradine had enough sense to swallow hard and nod.

Zach whistled his way back down the walk, giving the interested neighbor a wide smile and a wink.

Back at the office again, he called his sister, Serena, to ask about where to buy a top-quality bed and a sofa. Serena knew about things like that, and she was willing to help.

"You redecorating, big brother?" she asked curiously.

"They're not for me, they're for a friend."

Serena listed three different stores, and then told him which one she considered the best.

After that, he focused all his attention on the Solomen case.

The first step was to find out who all of Northwest Growers' suppliers were, and name all of them as co-defendants. The second step was to hire a private investigator who could work for Solomen as a truck driver. That would give Zach his independent-expert reports about the source of the contamination. On the strength of that, he'd launch a hefty countersuit against Northwest Growers, and Safefood, as well, for maligning Solomen's business reputation.

They'd need a date for the examination of discovery.

He pushed the intercom, feeling more excited about work than he'd felt since his first week of articling.

"Brenda, get Ozzie King on the phone for me, would you?"

Ozzie was an excellent investigator.

"Does this mean you've decided to defend Mr. Solomen, Mr. Jones?"

"It sure does, Brenda."

There was more warmth in her voice than he was accustomed to hearing. "Mr. Jones, I think that's such a wise decision. Mr. Solomen is such a nice man. I'll get King on the line for you right away, and if there's anything else I can do, just ask."

Zach stared at the intercom.

What the hell had come over Brenda?

HE'D TOLD JENNY he'd pick her up after her last class, which finished at six, and he barely made it. She was waiting outside the law building when he pulled up, and the warm, intimate smile she gave him when he stopped the car spoke of shared secrets.

He let his gaze wander over her.

She was wearing jeans and a shirt with a long green sweater over it. His gaze traveled down her body, knowing now the exact shape and feel of the firm, small breasts hidden under her blue shirt, and the enticing curve of waist and hip and thigh—only hinted at beneath the worn denim of her jeans.

He also knew how that soft, luxurious cloud of hair felt, spread across his naked chest.

Ahh, Jenny. My darling, sexy Jenny.

Desire swirled in him just looking at her. He couldn't remember ever being this turned-on by a woman before.

He got out and hurried over to her, taking her in his arms for a quick, thorough kiss before he led her back to the car.

"I thought of you all day," she confessed shyly, settling in the passenger seat. It pleased him to see the trace of color that rose in her skin when she told him that. But then she gave him a wicked sideways grin and added, "Mostly because I could hardly stay awake, and I figure it's at least half your fault. I've got to get to bed earlier than two if I'm going to be functional the next day."

He nodded in sober agreement. "Absolutely. I'll make sure you get to bed much earlier tonight." He growled deep in his throat. "In fact," he added hopefully, "if you're really tired, maybe we should skip dinner and go straight to bed now?"

Bright spots of color appeared in her cheeks. She gave him a long, considering look over the top of her glasses, but then she sat up a little straighter in the seat, shoved her frames farther up on her nose and shook her head, no, making wisps of bright hair tumble around her face. "Woman doesn't live by. . . bed alone. And I'm starving. I'd really like some food. Do you want me to make us something at my place?"

"At your place?" He thought of the mattress on the concrete floor, the sagging sofa, and bitter old Carradine with a stethoscope pressed against the upstairs floorboards.

"How about coming over to my apartment? You haven't seen it yet." It was the day his cleaning service came, so everything would be shining. And there was his own huge water bed on its secure frame. . . . Fantasies began forming.

"Do you have food there?"

Jenny definitely had a one-track mind when it came to food. He thought of his fridge, with its half quart of milk and seven cans of beer. "Not exactly, but we could pick up something on our way."

"Okay. But I need to go home first. I'd like to change. There was gum on the bench in the cafeteria this morning, and it's all over my jeans."

"How about I pick up some take-out Chinese food while you're changing?"

"Super. Get some of those big fat noodles, okay? I adore those. And lots of rice."

She was getting ready to slide out of the car the moment it stopped, but he held on to her arm. "Jenny."

"Yes, what?"

"Will you spend the night with me?"

She gave him that long, considering glance he was getting used to. "Yes," she said after a pause that nearly did him in. "I'd like that."

He let out the breath he'd been holding and gave her his best smile. "I'd like that, too." It was the understatement of the century. "And Jenny?"

"What?"

"Don't bother bringing pajamas."

She grinned and got out, trotting around the house to the basement door. The light was on in the basement, and she squinted up at it, feeling guilty. Surely she hadn't forgotten and left it on all day? She'd been in such a fog when she left this morning, it was possible. Funny, Amos hadn't come down and unscrewed the bulb, though. He was like a bird dog about lights left on.

Well, she'd turn it off as soon as she got the door open.

She'd just gotten her key in the lock, thinking she'd have time for a quick shower if she hurried, when Amos himself materialized like a wraith from the furnace area, giving her a start.

"Gosh, Amos, you scared me."

"I'd like a word with you."

Damn, just when she was in a hurry. An apprehensive knot clenched tight in her stomach. Undoubtedly he was going to lecture her about the light, and probably about Zach's car being parked in front of the house half the night, as well. He was such an old prude.

"Yes, Amos?"

She opened her door and stood blocking it, so maybe he'd have his say and get it over with fast. Maybe if she apologized. "I'm sorry about the light, Amos. I must have forgotten it this morning."

"I put in a new bulb, turned it on myself. Leave the derned thing be. Might as well leave it on all the time. Uses up more power turning it off and on, anyhow."

Well. Miracles actually happened, after all. They'd had more than enough discussions over that blasted light in the three years she'd lived here. And she'd used that very argument about turning it on and leaving it time and again herself with him, to no avail.

What was up with him today? He looked strange; his mouth was even more pinched in than usual. His voice was sour and abrupt, but his next words were astonishing. "There's painters coming Friday to do your apartment over."

"Painters?" It was about the last thing she expected, and she couldn't take it in all at once. "Painters? Like, walls and . . . and, my God, Amos, not just the bathroom . . . the whole thing?"

"That's what I said. And I'll be moving that chesterfield out. The bed, as well. I've . . . humph . . . decided to put in new ones."

"New ones?" She was sounding more and more like an echo, but she was dumbfounded by this.

Amos Carradine, who pinched every nickel three times, offering to upgrade her apartment to this extent? And put in new furniture? Something was not right here, however wonderful it sounded. The logical, horrible reason popped into her head, and she wailed, "Are you raising my rent, Amos? Because I told you, I can't afford to pay any more. I promised not to bug you about things, as long as—"

"Same rent. Count yourself lucky." The foul look he gave her didn't go along with his denial. He turned on his heel and stomped away before Jenny could say anything else.

In a daze, she went in and shut the door, leaning on it for a few minutes and looking around at the place where she'd lived for the past three years.

It was dingy, no doubt about that. Seeing it through Zach's eyes last night, it had looked pretty awful. It could have been depressing, but she'd never allowed it to be. But with a new coat of paint—would they fill the holes in the walls?

Amos had said painters, which meant he'd hired someone. Surely professionals would do something about the cracks and things.

She shook her head in amazement.

And the couch, that awful, saggy piece of furniture he glorified by calling a chesterfield. And the bed...

The bed. This had happened awfully soon after the bed collapsed with her and Zach in it.

On it. It was coincidental, Amos making these changes the day after that happened.

Could Zach have somehow...? No, that was ridiculous, she reasoned, tearing off her clothes and racing into the shower. There wasn't any way she could think of that Zach might have been responsible. How could he have been?

Don't look a gift horse in the mouth, Jenny, she cautioned herself. *Don't start imagining things. He's not going to get involved in your living arrangements. Be sensible, here.*

She soaped and rinsed, careful not to wet her hair, which had been washed that morning.

Colors. Was there any way Amos would let her choose the colors for the paint? Or dare she push him that one step further?

She would. Images of bright, clear, primary colors and the pleasure they'd give her on rainy mornings danced in rainbow images as she dried off. Sloshing on extravagant quantities of her cologne, she then scrabbled through her underwear drawer for clean panties and a nice bra, her mind half on the coming evening with Zach, half on the miracle that was going to occur in her apartment.

She paused for a moment, wondering what to wear tonight.

It didn't matter a whole lot, because she knew from the look in Zach's eyes that it wouldn't be long at all until she was naked.

The thought of being naked, in Zach's arms, made her shiver with delight. Even paint couldn't compete. She found a skirt and sweater that would do for school tomorrow, and wriggled into a pair of tights.

Her life was changing. She paused a moment, staring at herself in the mirror as she dabbed some lip gloss on and brushed her hair.

The paint on her walls would be permanent, once it was done.

But Zach... A knot tied itself into a hurtful coil in her stomach. Zach was strictly temporary. She knew that, and she had to keep reminding herself all the time not to get too used to having him in her life.

It was going to hurt awfully bad when he left and she was alone again. Could she bear it?

She straightened her shoulders and looked past the glasses, into her own eyes. She'd just have to live

GET 4 BOOKS

FREE

Return this card, and we'll send you 4 brand-new Harlequin Temptation® novels, absolutely *FREE!* We'll even pay the postage both ways!

We're making you this offer to introduce you to the benefits of the Harlequin Reader Service®: free home delivery of brand-new romance novels, **AND** at a saving of 30¢ apiece compared to the cover price!

Accepting these 4 free books places you under no obligation to continue. You may cancel at any time, even just after receiving your free shipment. If you do not cancel, every month, we'll send 4 more Harlequin Temptation® novels and bill you just $2.69* apiece—that's all!

Yes! Please send me my 4 free Harlequin Temptation® novels, as explained above.

Name

Address   Apt.

City   State   Zip

142 CIH ADGT (U-H-T-11/91)

*Terms and prices subject to change without notice. Offer limited to one per household and not valid to current Harlequin Temptation® subscribers.

Sales tax applicable in NY.
© 1990 Harlequin Enterprises Limited.
PRINTED IN CANADA

DETACH ALONG DOTTED LINE AND MAIL TODAY! – DETACH ALONG DOTTED LINE AND MAIL TODAY! – DETACH ALONG DOTTED LINE AND MAIL TODAY!

Get 4 Books FREE

SEE BACK OF CARD FOR DETAILS

FREE MYSTERY GIFT

We will be happy to send you a free bonus gift! To request it, please check here, and mail this reply card promptly!

Thank you!

DETACH ALONG DOTTED LINE AND MAIL TODAY! – DETACH ALONG DOTTED LINE AND MAIL TODAY! – DETACH ALONG DOTTED LINE AND MAIL TODAY!

through it, because there wasn't any alternative. Besides, she'd had lots of practice at living through unbearable events. Hadn't she?

There'd been her mother's death, her father's desertion, losing her husband. She'd lived through all of those.

And what was the point of spoiling today with worries over what the future held?

For the time being, she was going to pull a Scarlett O'Hara.

She'd think about the consequences tomorrow.

Tonight . . . Tonight belonged to her and Zach.

His knock sounded on the door, and she grabbed her backpack and her purse and danced across to open it.

"Ready, Jen?"

The way he looked at her made her feel special, as if she was pretty and sexy. Irresistible, even.

The light was still on in the hallway, and it gave her real pleasure to leave it on as she closed and locked the door behind her.

"Ready," she said, smiling up at him.

7

His apartment was at the top of a new glass-and-brick tower built to capture a view of the city and the bay, and it intimidated the life out of Jenny for the first hour.

One entire wall was window, and she felt as though she were looking down at a make-believe world. The city below looked small and manageable from up here; the view of the bay was like a picture-postcard scene created solely for this vista.

"You've got so much...stuff," she commented, turning from the window to gaze around the huge, lavishly furnished open area that encompassed living room, dining area, and at one end, a roomy, space-age kitchen.

There were brass lamps discreetly lighting expensively framed pictures, a huge oak desk against one wall, matching oak coffee tables conveniently placed, and not one but three overstuffed sofa units covered in brown corduroy, scattered with dozens of cushions in cream and softly muted shades of brown. Goose down, Jenny deduced when she poked one with a tentative finger.

"This place is so . . . big."

Zach seemed a trifle embarrassed. "Yeah. Well, I bought it as an investment, before construction had even started, so a unit didn't cost a third of what they cost now. And the furniture's mostly castoffs from home—things Mom had stored in the attics. I like old things—that was my great grandfather's desk. My sister, Serena, insisted I get the sofas recovered. They were in bad shape. And she came over and arranged things for me after I moved in. It wouldn't look like this if I'd had to do it. I don't know much about decorating."

"I didn't even know you had a sister." It was eerie, knowing that he had a mole just above his left buttock, yet not knowing that he had a sister. It brought home to her how much there was about him that she didn't have the foggiest clue about. "Do you have other sisters and brothers, as well?"

In so many ways they were strangers.

"No, just the two of us. Serena's four years younger than I am. She's freaking out at the thought of turning thirty next month—though she'd kill me if she knew I told anybody that."

She opened her mouth to ask when the birthday was, exactly, but before she could form the question, he answered it.

"November 15th." He walked over and tipped her chin up with a forefinger, planting a kiss on her lips. "And what does that tell you about Serena, Madam Astrologer?"

Her arms went around him automatically, and she drew in the wonderful smell of him—musky, male, with that touch of lemony deodorant or after-shave. As usual, he was wearing an impeccably tailored charcoal gray suit, soft blue-striped shirt, matching silk tie.

She tightened her arms around his midriff. It made her feel less strange, being held in the familiar security of his arms. She reached up and loosened his tie, then stood on tiptoe to kiss his chin.

"She's Scorpio. She's probably beautiful, proud and very confident."

He whistled and looked surprised. His arms tightened around her. "That pretty much describes Serena, all right. I'm beginning to think maybe there's something to this astrology business, after all."

Jenny gave him a small poke in the back for being condescending, but she didn't expand on her description of Serena.

"What does she do?"

"Serena?" He planted a kiss on her nose and stood back, shrugging out of his suit jacket, undoing the buttons on his sleeves and rolling the cuffs back so his strong forearms showed.

Funny, she'd never noticed with other men how sexy forearms could be, dusted with hair like that. . . .

"She's a psychiatrist, just finishing her residency."
Formidable.

Jenny was profoundly relieved that the chances of her ever meeting Serena Jones were minimal. Psychiatrists always made her feel as if her head were transparent; and she'd bet this Serena would want to look in every hidden corner of her mind—especially if she knew Jenny had anything to do with her big brother.

Zach had her in his arms again, and if he went on kissing her this way. . .

She made a heroic effort and managed to move away enough so that reason could operate.

"Zach, all that food you bought . . ." she managed to say.

"Right. It's gonna get cold. Let's eat." His voice was as unsteady as hers.

Together they set plates and forks out on the small dining table, and he opened the assortment of bags Jenny had helped him carry up, lifting out carton after carton of steaming Chinese food.

"You bought enough for an army!"

"Well, you said you were hungry. And I figured we'd need some left over for breakfast."

It struck her then—the full impact of being here with him, knowing they'd make love tonight, knowing that for the first time, she'd wake up beside him in the morning, in this fancy apartment that felt absolutely foreign to her, with this man whose suit had probably cost more than her entire wardrobe. What the heck was she doing, thinking this was how it should be?

She didn't belong here.

Her throat closed and she couldn't swallow. "Y'know, this . . . this scares me a little, Zach," she said in a choked voice, setting down her fork with the mouthful of noodles she'd been about to devour.

He didn't pretend not to understand what she meant. He looked across at her and set his fork down, too.

"Being here with me, you mean?" His voice was gentle.

She nodded, avoiding his eyes. "It's just that...well, since Nick died...I haven't...gotten too involved with anyone."

"I sort of guessed that." He smiled at her. "When the bed collapsed, you said you'd always been a quiet sleeper. I couldn't help but figure . . ."

"Yeah, well." She was blushing. She hadn't meant to be that obvious. "The thing is, you're so . . . different. I mean, really different than anyone else I know."

"So are you, Jenny. Wonderfully different."

"But . . . but, doesn't it . . . scare you a little? I mean, if you think about it, what have we really got in common? This apartment—it's more luxurious than anything I've ever seen. It makes me aware of . . . of all the spaces between us. You saw where I live."

He stood and came around the table, lifting her into his arms.

"The only spaces between us are the ones we allow to be there, Jenny." He slid an arm under her knees, swung her up in his arms, and set off down a hallway to his bedroom. She was aware of more spaciousness, of more heavy, old furniture. The room smelled of wax and his after-shave. She felt the immense bed undulate as he laid her on it. It was covered in something deep blue and soft.

His hands were quick and sure on her clothing, stripping it away. He undid the buttons on his shirt, and within seconds, he was naked, kneeling beside her on the gently moving surface.

"Jenny, I look at you and I see an outrageous, delightful woman who makes me laugh, who makes me crazy with wanting her. All day today, I didn't want to eat, or sleep, or work, or do any damned thing except this. This is where spaces between people don't really matter. And with us, like this, there aren't any here."

His lips trailed across her shoulder, his tongue creating a hot, wet path that made her shudder. "I'll prove to you there aren't any." He took her nipple into his mouth, drawing it deep, using subtle, knowing movements of his lips, and the heat that tingled between her thighs intensified to flame.

She moaned softly and reached up, wanting to draw him down on her, but he resisted. "Last night, darling Jenny, you led the way. Now it's my turn."

She could feel the strength of his arousal pressing against her side, and the heat and hardness made her desperate for him. She moved her hips, inviting, but he resisted, caressing her instead with his fingers, knowing the places that needed his touch, slipping into her wetness and out again in a rhythm that brought instant response from the depths of her body.

His lips explored her breasts, then slowly dipped lower until she could feel him trailing kisses down her stomach, descending languorously to the mound at her thighs.

For a moment, uncertainty came between her and sensation, and she reached down to touch his head, to hold him back.

"Zach, I don't . . . I've never . . ."

"Good. Now you'll belong only to me." The rough, raw passion in his voice thrilled her, and in another instant, his mouth and tongue found hidden parts of her, and there wasn't room for reluctance.

Her body arched and the bubble of need he'd created inside her exploded. She soared, lost in ecstasy.

He held her until the shuddering stilled, and then he entered her, long and slow, as if there was no urgency, no goal beyond the pleasure of flesh touching flesh; but she was aware again of his need, of the terrible effort he was making to hold back, to please only her.

"Now you," she whispered, using her body to lure him on. "Now you, Zach." She ran her hands down his warm, wet back, sliding them around, touching his belly, caressing.

But he wouldn't be drawn. Eyes shut tight, he held her still, fighting for control. His voice was shaky and hoarse. "Now, together, my lovely Jen. No spaces, remember?"

Slowly, ever so slowly, he began to excite her anew, in long, smooth sliding movements that paused at the brink of fulfillment—tantalizing, beckoning—and drew away.

She was full of him; filled and yet needing more; needing the increasing power of the surging joy he was creating once more in the deepest reaches of her body. She closed her eyes and hung on, beginning to move with him, unconsciously matching her rhythm to his. The tempo increased; the long, slow thrusts became more shallow.

She opened her eyes and he was above her, breath rasping in his throat, sweat slick on his features, shoulders bunched with muscle, intensity making the clean lines of his face almost gaunt.

At last, she was poised on the edge of the place they were seeking, overcome by the powerful waves of desire he stirred inside her.

"Zach?" Her voice sounded faint and faraway.

He understood. "Now, sweetheart. With me."

As one, they moved; and their voices joined as their bodies melded tightly to each other, sharing the rapture that they'd created together.

It was just as he'd promised. There were no spaces.

AFTER THAT NIGHT, they were together every moment they could steal from work or from university. The passion between them was like a potent drug, and they spent a fair amount of their time together experimenting with it, drunk with the sensual explosions they stirred in one another, eager only to be together, and alone.

Jenny blossomed during the next several weeks and Zach watched her, captivated by the aura of happiness and excitement that seemed to radiate from every pore of her body.

He'd never known a woman quite as alive as Jenny. She seemed to give off sparks of vitality.

Her unease at being in his apartment soon disappeared, and they spent marvelous hours together there, laughing and talking, watching the newest videos, almost always making love at some point, but also enjoying quiet times. Zach would work at his desk while Jenny studied, curled into a ball on one of the sofas. Afterward they'd sit outside on his small deck and watch the stars come out.

Jenny's ecstatic delight in the renovations to her basement suite gave Zach a special, secret pleasure. Carradine had grudgingly had the holes in the walls repaired, and a plumber corrected the leaking pipes that had stained the ceiling and warped the bathroom tile.

Jenny convinced Amos to let her choose the colors for the repainting job, and even Zach was amazed at the results. At her instruction, most of the walls and all the ceilings were done a basic pale eggshell, which made the entire place seem much larger and brighter than before, but in each area, Jenny had also chosen a dramatic splash of primary color for one feature wall.

The area behind her small kitchen table was daffodil, so that it seemed the sun was shining in even on the dullest mornings. In the tiny bathroom, blush pink created a feeling of warmth and space on the wall opposite the shower. In the bedroom, cornflower blue covered the wall behind the new double bed.

Zach loved that bed. He'd chosen it and the navy blue sofa, and had had them delivered, as he'd told Carradine he would. He made certain the bed had the finest mattress money could buy; no more plywood and loose blocks for Jenny.

He'd wanted to get a queen size, but the room proved too small, and after spending several delicious nights on the double, he was glad it had worked out that way. Less space meant they had to stay closely locked in one another's arms, and that suited him just fine.

Most things suited him these days—except the disagreements he and Jenny got into over her clients from the legal-aid clinic.

Three times in a single week, they'd been making love in Jenny's bedroom when the telephone rang late at night. Jenny only had one phone, and it was in the other room.

The first time, Zach could only assume that it was bad news—someone dead or in an accident. He'd grabbed a blanket and taken it to wrap around her bare shoulders, holding her against his warm body for a long moment to comfort her if he could. But Jenny didn't seem to be noticeably upset, so Zach finally went back to bed.

As Jenny told him half an hour later when she crawled back into bed and put her cold feet on his legs, the caller was Veronica Glickman.

"Glickman?" Zach was astonished. "How the hell did she get your home number?"

"Oh, I gave it to her when she was so worried about her house being condemned," Jenny said serenely. "It's hard to get in touch with her. She doesn't have a phone, so she had to call me. There wasn't any other way to talk with her."

Zach was disturbed. "You shouldn't ever give those people your home number, Jen. It's not professional. What was the emergency tonight with Glickman, calling you at this hour?"

Jenny snuggled close to him, her cold hands warming fast on his thighs. "No emergency. She was just lonely and wanted to talk. She was calling from the lobby of some hotel."

Some bar, Zach thought, but he didn't say it, because Jenny's hands were much warmer now, and they were stroking a part of him that responded instantly to being stroked. A moment later, he'd entirely forgotten Veronica Glickman, because Jenny had rolled on top of him and taken him inside her warm, wet depths.

TWO NIGHTS LATER, they were again involved in a crucial maneuver when the phone began to ring. This time, they tried to ignore the strident summons, but neither succeeded. At last, Jenny staggered out of bed, located her glasses and hurried into the other room.

Again, it was Veronica Glickman.

This time, Zach was more vocal about it. They had what amounted to an argument; but it was hard to stay annoyed with one another when they were both naked. And the bed wasn't that big, so they couldn't really avoid touching.

The third time, however, they had an outright quarrel over Veronica's call. It came at two in the morning, startling them both out of sleep. Jenny was half frozen when she came back to bed, and Zach was furious.

"You've got to tell that bloody woman to stop calling you here. Either that or get your number changed."

He hadn't expected Jenny to get angry, but she did. She'd been cuddled next to him, and she jerked away, as far as the bed allowed, her small body taut with outrage.

"That bloody woman, as you call her, happens to be lonely, and if she wants to call me, that's between her and me. You don't understand the first thing about loneliness. How could you—surrounded all the time by your family and your friends?"

This was true, he had to admit. He'd never been really lonely that he could remember. He apologized, and Jenny relented, but it left a residue of bad feeling between them, because he still felt Jenny was making a huge mistake, encouraging Veronica.

THE TROUBLE WAS, Jenny treated all her clients as if they were her friends, and it was causing Zach untold problems at the Thursday-evening legal-advice clinic.

As usual, the area smelled of stale coffee, wet overcoats and cheap perfume when he arrived that Thursday evening.

Tonight must be the sixth clinic he'd supervised, Zach reflected wearily, and he wished to God he'd stopped while he was ahead and quit coming here after the first two. Not that he minded helping the students; he actually found it enjoyable.

It wasn't the questions or the decisions that bothered him. It was this whole thing with Jenny and her street people. It was getting out of control. It was driving the assistants crazy and irritating the hell out of the other students.

One of the assistants hurried over to him as he was taking off his raincoat. Jenny had already settled in at her assigned table, and was talking with someone.

The assistant motioned to the long line of people waiting to be seen, and she sounded annoyed. "At least half of these people only want to see Ms. Lathrop, Mr. Jones, and I don't know how to handle it. If I tell them they have to see whoever they're assigned to, they simply say they'll wait till Miss Jenny's free. That's what they call her—Miss Jenny. What should I do about it, Mr. Jones?"

He was damned if he knew. Zach heard them himself, the bag ladies and derelicts, all asking for Miss Jenny. To begin with, it was totally unprofessional, letting these people call her by her first name. He'd spoken to her about it several times, reemphasizing the need for professionalism, for distancing oneself from the client. Obviously, he was going to have to bring it up again.

He tried hard not to make any exceptions as far as the clinic was concerned in his dealings with her, although from glances and overheard remarks, he knew the other students had guessed long ago that there was something going on between them.

Difficult as it was, Zach really tried to be as professional as possible while he was here.

"Ask Ms. Lathrop to come over when she's free."

He found a comparatively quiet corner and waited. In a few moments, Jenny hurried over, her hair ablaze and coming loose from its bun, glasses falling off her nose, prim black shirt and calf-length printed skirt hiding her long legs. He knew she was wearing pink lace panties under her dark panty hose—panties he'd bought her.

He shouldn't watch her dress when they were coming here. It made everything that much tougher. He wanted to run a hand up under her skirt, tug the panty hose down— He felt his body grow hard, and he forced himself to pay attention to the business at hand.

"Ms. Lathrop, why are all these people calling you by your first name? You understand the importance of a professional approach. And the assistants are complaining because too many people insist on seeing only you."

That sounded pedantic and accusatory and petty. But what the hell? He was doing the best he could under impossible circumstances. He studiously avoided looking at her legs, but that left her breasts, and he also knew she wasn't wearing a bra under the damned shirt. She'd asked him whether or not her nipples showed before they left, and he'd assured her they didn't.

Now he wished he'd made her wear long underwear.

Jenny shoved her glasses higher on her nose and glared at him. "It's Veronica's fault they all want to talk to me. She sits out there every Thursday night and goes on and on about me. I hate it as much as everybody else. My caseload is killing me. And I always start out professional with them. For gosh sakes, Zach, take a look at these people. They need some human contact. They already feel the whole world looks down on them. If it makes them more comfortable to call me Miss Jenny, I can't see what harm it does. At least they say 'Miss.'"

"But you know it's a mistake to become personally involved on any level with a client, Ms. Lathrop," Zach reiterated patiently, for what seemed like the twentieth time. "A client is a problem with a rational solution. You can't allow yourself to relate on any level except that one. The practice of law is a legal affair, not an emotional issue."

She gave him a defiantly stubborn look—a look Zach had come to recognize uncomfortably—and dread.

"That's bullshit, Zach. Maybe you can practice law from an ivory tower, but I can't. To me, clients are people first, problems second. That's what makes being a lawyer fun. Why don't you try talking to some of these people for a change? Try relating on a human level instead of categorizing them as problems. And for God's sake, stop calling me Ms. Lathrop. You're the only person here who does, and it's ridiculous."

She turned and hurried back to her table, leaving Zach with an overwhelming urge to rush over and strangle her. She managed to make him feel guilty and snobbish and simpleminded all in one bundle.

The simple truth was, he raged to himself, he didn't want to talk with Jenny's people. The particular type of clients she attracted made him uneasy. He'd never in a million years admit it to her, but he'd always privately called them the "window people."

Before Jenny, he used to sit in expensive restaurants and see them pass by, always through the window. He felt sorry for them, he gave generously to community fund-raising drives aimed at providing shelters and food. But they had their life, he had his; it was just the way things operated.

Now, because of Jenny, he was being introduced to them, being drawn into their problems, being awakened at night by their phone calls, consulted about impossible situations he really had no idea how to handle. Technically, the things they talked to Jenny about more often than not weren't legal problems with clear-cut solutions at all. Or if they were, they were cases Zach wouldn't touch with a ten-foot pole.

Like the case of Elias Redthorn, for example.

The clinic was more than half over that evening when Jenny waved Zach over to her table. Zach had noticed the small, rather repulsive man in the heavy body brace; he'd been the one having an impassioned discussion with Veronica Glickman during the entire first half of the clinic. Veronica was undoubtedly the reason he'd refused to see the student he was assigned to, choosing instead to wait over an hour until Jenny was free.

He was now sitting on the wooden client's chair in front of her desk, with what Zach could only describe as a hangdog look on his long face.

Jenny introduced Zach, and the little man struggled to his feet to shake hands. Zach noticed that besides the cumbersome body brace, Redthorn wore a heavy orthopedic shoe on one foot, which was built up at least six inches. He shook the soft, sweaty paw the man extended, feeling a surge of pity but also feeling irritated by the obsequious way Redthorn acted and spoke.

"I need a bit of advice, Zach," Jenny began in an animated voice. She'd obviously forgotten the earlier scene. "Elias has a complex problem here. His car—"

Redthorn interrupted her. "It's an '82 Oldsmobile," he said, rubbing his palms together and smacking his lips in a way that set Zach's teeth on edge. "Mint condition. At least, it was before the accident."

Jenny took up the story again. "Elias's car was stolen two weeks ago. The police recovered it after a couple of days, and returned it to Elias, but they neglected to check it mechanically, to make sure it hadn't sustained damage while it was stolen."

Again Elias interrupted, in a pitiful nasal whine. "I've had it two years, that car. Nary a scratch on it. I keep it covered when I'm not using it." He cast what was obviously intended to be an appealing, pathetic look at Zach. "Not easy for someone like me to afford a car, y'see, gov'ner. Born with my leg like this, I was. Never got much schooling. Hard to find a steady job when you're a cripple, gov'ner, don't you agree?"

Zach had no idea what the hell to say to a question like that. He was feeling more and more uncomfortable. He shot Jenny a pleading glance, and she hurriedly took up the tale again.

"Elias took the car out for a drive, and it went out of control, even though he was trying to use the brakes." She referred now to a printed sheet in front of her. "It ran into a parked vehicle and then a lamppost. This report says there was extensive damage to both vehicles, and the post was sheared off at the base." She looked up, her blue eyes filled with righteous outrage. "Elias's back was injured, and now he's forced to wear that brace, perhaps permanently. And the police are charging him with undue care and attention, as well as dangerous driving. Can you believe it?"

"Never had an accident before, gov'ner. Very particular about my driving, I am."

Zach wished he would shut up. His voice grated like nails on a blackboard.

Zach tried to forget Redthorn and consider the problem here. "It shouldn't be too difficult to have the charge dismissed, if the police did in fact return the vehicle without having it thoroughly checked," he suggested.

Jenny waved a hand, brushing that aside. "Absolutely. That's exactly what I intend to do. No problem there. I've already told Elias that. What I wanted to consult you about is whether or not Elias has a case against the police force. He feels—and I think he's right—that he should receive a substantial settlement because of the injury he's sustained."

It was beginning to dawn on Zach that there was more here than he wanted to deal with. He felt a peculiar sinking sensation in his stomach as the ramifications of the thing became clear.

He and Jenny both knew that because she was still a student, she couldn't handle cases involving personal injury. They also both knew that Zach's firm handled this sort of thing all the time. Therefore . . .

Zach knew without a shadow of a doubt that his partners would turn thumbs down on this one without any deliberation at all. The chances of winning were minimal, the time involved in preparation would be major, and the client was indigent, so the work would be *pro bono*. For free.

He already had them embroiled in the Solomen case, against their better judgment.

They'd never agree to taking on Redthorn. They'd likely have Zach committed to a mental institution if he even brought it up. It would take only two doctors to accomplish that and Ken Meredith played squash with all the residents from Vancouver General Hospital.

Zach opened his mouth to tell Jenny she was flogging a very dead horse, and closed it again because of Redthorn's presence.

"I told Elias I was sure your firm would consider this a matter of moral conscience," she added with her sweetest smile, giving her glasses a triumphant poke and Zach a wide-eyed, hopeful look.

Zach managed what he prayed was a noncommittal noise in his throat before he made his escape. He must be developing some psychic ability, because for the first time in his life he could see the immediate future.

It was black—excessively black—shot through with nasty streaks of angry red.

8

"I JUST CAN'T BELIEVE your firm could be this callous!" Jenny's voice was trembling with outrage and increasing in volume, and several heads turned their way. "It reminds me all over again of what happened when Nick was killed—how we were all treated like second-class citizens just because we didn't have money behind us!"

The quietly luxurious dining room at the William Tell wasn't exactly the place to have a disagreement, Zach realized. A soft violin concerto discreetly playing in the background didn't muffle anything except murmurs, and Jenny wasn't exactly murmuring.

"If you had a shred of feeling for those less fortunate than yourself, you wouldn't hesitate to take Elias's case."

"Look, I'm sick of hearing about Elias Redthorn, okay?"

Zach was also more than a little tired of hearing about Jenny's dead husband, when it came right down to it—although he didn't say so. How the hell could he hope to compete with a dead man, for cripes' sake?

Zach made a conscious effort to lower his voice. "Look, Jenny, you're suggesting my firm sue the Vancouver Police Department. That's a serious undertaking. The firm's always been on the best of terms with them—we rely on their cooperation."

She rolled her eyes, silently expressing her disgust with that attitude.

"You've got to admit, Jenny, it's not even an open-and-shut case. This Redthorn guy—"

The waiter, face impassive, appeared at Zach's shoulder and ceremoniously picked up the bottle of wine Zach had optimistically ordered. He refilled their glasses.

Jenny's was still full. Zach emptied his so as to give the guy something to do and the waiter filled it again, emptying the bottle.

"Another bottle, sir?"

"No. No, thanks, that's enough."

"Very good, sir."

Zach decided he was also disillusioned with the William Tell, a place he'd always enjoyed till tonight. He'd counted, maybe just a trifle callously, on these elite surroundings to help him out with this discussion with Jenny, assuming—wrongly, as it turned out—that she'd be too intimidated by the five waiters, two busboys, haughty wine steward and stiffly formal maître d' hovering over and around their table to create a major scene over the damned Redthorn affair.

Well, he'd been wrong before. He'd just never been quite this wrong, this publicly.

He tried sweet reason. "Jenny, I don't run the firm by myself. It's a partnership, and when both other partners decide against taking a case, there's not a hell of a lot I can do."

She gave him a fiery glare over the top of her glasses. "You could set an example. You could threaten to leave the firm, on principle. You could take the case independently of the firm."

He was trying to control his anger, but it put a hard edge in his voice. "For Christ's sake, Jenny, do you understand what you're suggesting? I helped found the firm, I'm a partner. I'm not about to leave. That's the most unreasonable thing I've ever heard."

She sniffed and then stared down at her dinner for several long moments and when she looked up at him again there was less anger in her face. "I guess it is unreasonable," she admitted. "But the whole thing seems so unfair to me. You saw Elias, in that horrible body cast, with his built-up shoe. And he's dirt-poor. That's what this is really about, isn't it? If Elias had money, you'd take the case, right?"

"Not necessarily, no." Zach had to admit to himself, reluctantly, that it might be a lot more probable, though. "Look, Jenny, unfortunately firms like ours are out there to make money. This is a competitive business. You know how many legal firms go under each year. We have to be hardheaded about what we do."

She toyed with her seafood salad. "Ruthless," she said after a while, and there was a sad, weary acceptance in her tone. "You have to be ruthless, and people like Elias Redthorn are always the innocent victims."

Zach was silent. He was worn-out from arguing with her, and still smarting from the scene with Ken and Derek that afternoon, when he'd rashly proposed the Redthorn case to them. It had been nothing short of humiliating.

They'd told him in no uncertain terms they figured he was flipping out. First the Solomen thing, and now this? They'd suggested a nice long holiday, preferably at a mental-health facility, just as he'd figured they would.

Although he'd been unusually reticent about Jenny, they said they'd already guessed there was something going on in his life that was affecting his brain, and they figured it had a lot to do with another part of his body. They reminded him that he'd canceled squash games, avoided the usual weekend pub crawl, turned down a date with Ken's cousin's cousin from Oakland—a real, live honest-to-God California girl, blond and buxom and reportedly mad about Vancouver lawyers. To say nothing of volunteering for the entire semester at the legal-advice clinic. Which just might, Zach, old buddy, old pal, old rascal, have something to do with this new attitude. Right?

Nudge, nudge. Wink, wink.

Zach had deflected their pointed remarks about female law students, which of course was a dead giveaway.

The strange thing was, he'd never had the slightest desire before to conceal his love life from them. It hadn't mattered one whit to him, having his friends know he was sleeping with a new lady.

So why did it matter like hell this time?

Because it was Jenny.

He looked across the table at her. She was wearing a green dress with a soft, open neckline—a dress that clung to her breasts, her waist, her hips, then flared out gracefully at the hem. Her beautiful, shining hair was caught up in a high knot on top of her head, with some cascading down her back and wisps trailing over her forehead and in front of her ears. Her blue eyes were huge behind her glasses, and her freckles looked like little golden dots across her nose and cheeks.

A rush of feeling swept over him—regret that they were fighting, a surge of the intense physical desire he always experienced when he was near her, and another emotion—a tender, protective combination of confused, exasperated responses he wasn't ready to explore right now.

The truth was, he no longer saw Jenny objectively, he realized. He saw a woman who captivated him, whose body he knew intimately and adored, whose mind he admired, but whose convictions made him want to shake her until her brains rattled.

Nope, he wasn't the least bit objective about her. That was certain.

What he felt for Jenny was different from anything he'd ever felt before about a woman. If one of his partners today had dared make a remark less than respectful about her, he'd have broken that partner's nose without hesitating, friend or no friend. Whatever this was between him and Jenny, he needed to sort it out by himself.

"Would you like some dessert, sir?"

The waiters had cleared away their half-eaten plates of food, and their coffee steamed untouched in china cups.

"Jenny? Dessert?"

"No, thanks. Nothing more. I think I'd like to go home now, Zach." She was subdued and formal—not at all her usual, fiery self.

He paid the bill and they went out into the soft, rainy night. The valet service already had his car waiting under the awning. Zach gave him a tip, and soon they were idling their way through the crowded Friday-night streets.

Jenny was quiet, and Zach's mind kept replaying parts of their conversation.

"Jenny, what was your husband like?" The question seemed to pop out of his mouth of its own accord.

She turned and gave him a puzzled glance. "Nick? You want to know what Nick was like? Why, Zach?"

He struggled for words. "I . . . I guess I feel as if he's there between us all the time, that you're . . . comparing me to him, or something."

And finding me wanting, he added silently.

She turned away from him and looked out the window. "That's crazy. I'd never do that. You're very different from him. There's no basis for comparison at all."

He waited, but she didn't say anything more, and the tension that had been growing between them all evening increased.

"You want to go to your place, or mine?"

"Mine, I think. I've got a ton of homework to do."

"It's Friday. You've got the whole damned weekend to do your homework." He knew he sounded grouchy, and he didn't give a damn. She was pushing him.

"I still want to go home."

Zach stepped hard on the gas, and the powerful little car surged ahead, darting between a bus and a delivery truck with an inch to spare on either side.

She wanted to go home, he'd take her home.

JENNY KNEW HE WAS MAD at her. It was obvious from his clenched jaw and the way he was driving. She knew she'd been less than pleasant company tonight, raging at him in that fancy restaurant.

C'mon. Be honest, Jenny. You were an out-and-out bitch, and you know it. And you also know it wasn't all because of Elias Redthorn.

It was herself she was really angry with. Why in God's name had she let herself get this involved with Zachary Jones? She'd known from the first moment she'd laid eyes on him, in the Legal Clinic that night, that Jenny Lathrop and Zachary Jones might as well inhabit different planets, for all they had in common.

And knowing that, what had she done? She'd ambled along like a sheep to a slaughter and let herself fall in love with him. Well, maybe not like a sheep, exactly. Vivid memories of her avid seduction attempt contradicted the sheep analogy. *Love* was the operative word here, with a capital letter *L*, because she wasn't just a little in love; this wasn't a passing fancy, a here-today-gone-tomorrow liaison.

Nope, she'd gone the whole nine yards here. She actually had fantasies about having his babies, growing old with him, arguing with him over legal affairs until they were both too senile to know a writ of habeas corpus from a subpoena. And there wasn't a snowball's chance in hell of that ever happening; she'd known that from the beginning. So how stupid could a smart woman get, anyway?

He pulled up in front of the house, and without a word got out and came around to help her out. He had impeccable manners, even when he was furious.

He stalked behind her to the basement door, picked up the key when she dropped it, and opened the lock. Her glasses were covered in raindrops and she couldn't see his face clearly, but she knew he wasn't going to come in with her.

Panic gripped her, even though her brain knew the best thing that could happen was for him to walk out of her life right now, before things got even worse.

Better? That was the whole point. She could deal with "worse"; she'd been dealing with it most of her life. It was "better" she couldn't handle.

"Jenny." His voice was businesslike, impersonal. He was standing just inside the basement entrance, not touching her, his elegant raincoat dripping on the cement. The light that was always on now shone down on his stern features.

"Yes, Zach?" She was proud of the way she kept her own voice under control.

He was about to say goodbye, it's been difficult knowing you. And surely she could get through the few minutes it took without bursting into tears or screaming and throwing herself on him or anything nutty like that. There'd be plenty of time for tears later....

"I was talking to my mother today, and she'd like to meet you. She's asked us to come for dinner tomorrow."

JENNY KNEW SHE WAS wearing the wrong thing, but there was some consolation in realizing that not a single garment in her closet would have been right, anyway. As it was, she'd changed four times before settling on the blue corduroy skirt, navy tights and plain white shirt she was wearing. Catching sight of herself in a fulllength mirror in the entrance hall a moment ago, she'd realized too late that she looked like a schoolgirl in uniform. She'd even braided her hair—a French braid that she'd taken out seven times before she got it right.

"I THINK IT'S WARM ENOUGH to sit out on the deck, don't you, Serena?" Zach's mother, Lucille Jones, wasn't at all what Jenny had expected.

She was short and rather plump, with beautiful, deep-set hazel eyes and silvery blond hair. She ushered Jenny through one elegantly decorated room after the other, then out through sliding-glass doors onto a ground-level cedar deck.

Jenny surveyed the backyard. The place was like a park, for God's sake. Nearby was a swimming pool and a cabana. Beyond that was a tennis court.

"Eva dried the chairs off this morning after all that rain. Now the sun's out, we might as well take advantage of it. Jenny, you have glorious hair, dear. I always longed for hair like yours."

"Thank you, Mrs. Jones."

"Heavens, call me Lucille. Mrs. Jones makes me feel quite ancient."

Jenny had only been around Lucille Jones for fifteen minutes, and she liked the older woman, despite her prejudices. It would have been difficult not to like her; she'd greeted Jenny with a warm hug and an easy, sincere welcome. It was apparent she adored her tall son; she tugged him down to her level to plant a huge, noisy kiss on his cheek.

Zach's sister, Serena, on the other hand, was everything Jenny had been afraid she would be. Tall and model-slim, with honey-blond hair drawn back in the kind of elegant knot Jenny could never seem to manage, Serena was poised and coolly beautiful. Her low, husky voice was perfectly modulated. Her green eyes, like Zach's in color only, seemed to bore into Jenny mercilessly. Like Jenny, she was wearing a simple skirt and blouse, but hers bore not the slightest resemblance to any kind of uniform. The dramatic scarlet silk shirt and matching wool skirt, the simple silver chains and oversize hoop earrings made a fashion statement Jenny wouldn't know how to begin to emulate—even if she could afford to.

And on top of all that, Serena was a psychiatrist. Jenny tried to swallow the dry, hard lump in her throat and reminded herself that she wasn't a weird hippie kid any longer. She was a lawyer. Well, she would be in a matter of months.

Eventually they were seated around a glass-topped table. Even having Zach sit next to her and take her hand firmly in his didn't help Jenny much.

Serena scared her silly. The size and opulence of this damned mansion scared her silly, when it came down to it. It was probably lucky Zach's father wasn't around yet, or he'd scare her silly, as well. She was ashamed of herself for being such a coward, but it didn't change how she felt. She actually could feel her knees trembling in their damned navy tights.

"You're a lawyer, Jenny?" Serena's polite question sounded like the beginning of an inquisition to Jenny.

"Not yet. I'm a third-year student."

"Oh? And have you decided yet where you'll be articling?"

"I've had interviews and offers from several firms. There's one firm out in New Westminster I think I'd like. They had toys for kids in the waiting room."

"Toys?" Serena's smooth brow wrinkled ever so slightly. "I'm afraid I don't see what toys have to do with articling."

"I figure a firm that cares about kids cares about people in general. That's what the law's really about, isn't it? People."

Serena was looking at her as if she were exhibiting signs of mental aberration.

A tall, angular woman came out the sliding doors and over to them. "You having drinks, or tea, or what, Ms. Lucille? Zachary, hello there. About time you came to see us. You need a haircut, young man."

Zach got to his feet and went over to give the woman an affectionate hug, leading her over to where Jenny was sitting. "Eva, I'd like you to meet Jenny Lathrop. Jenny, Eva Kramer."

Jenny got to her feet and shook hands. Eva's narrow dark eyes assessed her thoroughly, and then she smiled at her.

Jenny refused a drink, choosing tea instead, and Lucille went off with Eva to help bring a tray.

"Is your family from Vancouver, Jenny?" Serena was on the trail again, and Jenny drew in a deep breath. She might just as well lay out the facts about herself like playing cards, faceup, right now, and let Serena draw her own conclusions. It would stop all this verbal fencing, and she had nothing she needed to hide.

Zach had her hand again, and she felt the reassuring warmth of his strong fingers around her own. She turned slightly, meeting Serena's disconcerting gaze head on.

"My mother's dead," she began, "and my father's somewhere in Mexico, I don't know exactly where. I grew up on a farming commune...."

THEY WERE BACK in Jenny's apartment late that night, with the lights out, the door locked, and snuggled down amid the blankets.

Jenny traced the hard planes of Zach's face with her hand, loving the feel of his muscular arm beneath her head, the weight of his leg across her thighs. The loving had been tumultuous, and they lingered in its afterglow, feeling peaceful and lethargic.

"You look like your dad, but you're a lot more relaxed than he is. Is he always that dressed up, or was it just because I was there, Zach?"

His voice was slow, lazy and drugged with recent passion. "He's always like that. I used to wish when I was a kid that he'd come out and throw a football with me, like some of the other kids' dads did. But it's tough to play football in a three-piece suit. Dad's a lawyer, through and through. He doesn't know any other way to be. It was Eva's husband, Karl, who taught me things like how to throw a football and fix a bicycle." With a sad note in his voice, he added, "Karl died a few years ago. I still miss him."

"So Eva's been with your family for a long time?"

"Ever since I was a baby. Technically, she's our housekeeper, but she and Mom are also good friends. And she's like a second mother to Serena and me."

"I love your mom." Her fingers traced the outline of his ear. She hadn't expected it to happen; she'd been a wreck at the thought of meeting his mother. And then Lucille had charmed her, put her at ease. "She's the kind of mother everybody needs—so warm and approving and affectionate."

It was Serena and Theodore Jones she ought to have been apprehensive about.

Zach was like his mother, Jenny reflected. And Serena—Jenny snuggled deeper into the cave of blankets, feeling suddenly chilled. Serena was exactly like her father: stiff, formal, seemingly unable to show any trace of human emotion.

"What was your mom like, Jenny? You never really say what your parents were like, you know. You skip the details."

She realized that was true. He'd taken her home to meet his family; surely he deserved a closer look at hers?

"You want to see some pictures of them? I've got some somewhere." She wriggled out of his arms and turned on the bedside light, pulling a cheap black cardboard album out of a dresser drawer. He punched the pillows into shape behind them and wrapped a quilt around their shoulders against the nighttime chill of the room.

The pictures seemed old, like moments from long ago frozen in time.

"This was when Mom and Dad were married. They waited until I was four before they made it legal. I told you they were hippies. That's me, with the flowers."

It was taken in a grassy field. A young and beautiful woman, fragile in a flowing Indian-style dress, and wearing a beaded headband low on her forehead, stood looking up at the tall, thin man with the luxuriant beard standing beside her. Her thick hair fell in loose waves past her waist. They held hands—the man and woman.

The child who had been Jenny, bare-legged and chubby, clutched a fistful of wildflowers and leaned against her father's leg, somehow outside the invisible circle the other two had drawn. Her smile and her father's were identical.

"What're their names?"

"My mother was Clara. My dad's name's Jacob. Jacob Neilson."

"She's very beautiful, your mother. You look like her," Zach commented gallantly, but Jenny shook her head.

"Don't flatter me. I look more like my dad. It sounds weird, probably, but I never knew my mother all that well. She was always off in her own world, meditating or reading or teaching people about herbs and plants, or working out astrological charts. She was always busy, and she never seemed to want to be bothered with me much. People were attracted to her, because she was so pretty, and there were always friends around her. Somehow I got lost in the shuffle." She shrugged. "But living on a commune, there were other women around who took me under their wing, so I wasn't the least bit deprived."

"Were you closer to your father?" Zach was turning the album's pages, stopping at a picture of a smiling group of long-haired people, gathered around a rough-hewn table at Christmastime.

"Not really. He was a dreamer. He was trained as a typesetter, but all he really wanted to do was write poetry. The center of his universe was my mother. He loved her so much, there wasn't room for anyone else. He was brokenhearted when she died. I think that's why he stays in Mexico, because there's nothing there to remind him of her."

"Do you miss him?"

She met his eyes and nodded—a slow, silent acknowledgment that touched his soul. "I wish things were different between him and me. I used to wish I was part of a huge, close family instead of being an only child."

She pointed to the picture he was looking at. "These people were sort of like my family, I guess. They lived with us on the farm. Other people came and went over the years, but Mary, Sergio, Janet and Bob were always there while I was growing up. Janet's daughter and I were the same age. Her name's Ilona. They all live in New Zealand now. They emigrated and bought a sheep ranch. I still keep in touch with them. This is me, here, beside Uncle Bill." She pointed to a wizened little old man, bald, with huge ears and a crooked grin. Standing beside him, Jenny was gangly now, with glasses perched on her nose. The old man's arm was around her shoulders.

"He was Janet's uncle. She rescued him out of a state nursing home when he was seventy-two and brought him to live with us. You had Karl, I had Uncle Bill. He taught me how to cook. He was fabulous in the kitchen. He'd owned a delicatessen when he was young—lost it to a crooked partner. He lived to ninety-three."

Zach turned the pages, and Jenny saw herself through his eyes, turning from a little girl into a bespectacled teen, awkward and ill at ease. Toward the end of the album was her wedding picture.

Nick, not much taller than Jenny and looking uncomfortable in the new suit he'd bought for the wedding, smiled out at them shyly, holding Jenny's hand in his. She was wearing an Empire-waisted long white dress with embroidery around the hem.

"Nick was twenty-one here, I was seventeen. I can't believe how young we were. If I had kids, I'd never want them marrying that young," she said thoughtfully, staring down at the photo. "I mean, at that age I didn't even know what was possible yet. I didn't know how different I'd be when I got older. Back then, I'd never have dared to even dream of being a lawyer. Nick would have laughed if I'd suggested it."

"Wouldn't he have been supportive of you?"

She thought about it, then shook her head. "I don't think so. He came from a traditional family. His father worked, his mother raised the kids, and that's how he figured it should be. I always had some kind of job after we were married, but Nick was never very happy about it. We needed the money, though, because his jobs in construction weren't steady. But for me to have pursued a career as a lawyer . . ." She considered it, and smiled sadly. "He'd have fought it. It would have made him feel inferior." She looked up into his eyes. "He wasn't self-assured, the way you are, Zach. He was gentle and kind, but he didn't have much education, and he didn't read a lot, either."

She looked down again, at the album. "I've often thought that if Nick had lived, we'd probably have been divorced by now," she said sadly. "We weren't well suited at all. He was the first boyfriend I ever had. How did I know what to look for in a husband?"

"Do you now, Jenny?" His voice was low, and there was a strange catch in it.

Jenny's heart skipped a beat. All of a sudden, she realized she was on dangerous ground here. She'd been babbling away, not realizing where this conversation was leading.

"I'm not looking for one now," she managed to say lightly. "I enjoy being on my own. Besides, what kind of life would the poor guy have? You know yourself how little time there is when you're a student. And then articling—I've heard you only work ten or twelve hours a day, if you're lucky. He'd be stuck with all the cooking and cleaning. And in case you haven't noticed, I can get pretty bad-tempered at times."

He didn't say anything. She could feel his warm breath on the side of her neck, his leg touching hers under the covers.

Almost like a reprieve, the telephone began to ring in the next room. Jenny scrambled off the bed and dragged her flannelette gown on over her head, feeling absurdly relieved by the interruption.

"You go to sleep," she said, pulling his socks over her bare feet. "It's probably Veronica. She's the only one who ever calls me this late. I'll try to get rid of her, but it's liable to take a while."

She hoped fervently that when she was gone he'd forget what they'd been talking about.

Zach lay with his arms behind his head, hearing the low mumble of Jenny's voice from the other room. The album was closed, resting on her pillow, but the images were clear in his mind.

It had answered so many of his questions, that album; laid to rest a lot of things he'd wondered about. But there were other questions it hadn't answered fully.

The image of the little girl, leaning against her father's leg, came to him clearly, and compassion for that child filled him. Even in the picture, Clara and Jacob formed an inner circle that Jenny wasn't part of.

It was hard to imagine what her childhood had been like. He had only his own to compare it with—private schools, Karl picking him up every day, his mother and

Eva loving him—spoiling him, when it came right down to it.

It sounded to him as if Jenny hadn't been spoiled at all; or even loved the way she ought to have been—the way he and Serena had been loved. Stiff as his father was, Zach had never doubted Theodore Jones's devotion to his children. His father was like a rock that the family rested upon: always there, always reliable.

Jenny had described her father as a dreamer. Dreamers were nice, but they weren't necessarily reliable.

And Nick Lathrop, the rather ordinary man whom Jenny had been married to for six long years . . .

In his mind, Zach had been gradually building Jenny's dead husband into a paragon of men, better at everything than Zach could ever be. The wedding picture and Jenny's blunt words had rectified that impression. As Jenny had said, there was nothing similar between Nick Lathrop and himself. There was no basis for comparison, good or bad, because they were different people.

It was comforting knowing that, believing it.

Today had been a landmark day in many ways. Jenny was the first woman he'd deliberately taken home to meet his family. Not that he needed or wanted their approval; it was simply a way of letting Jenny get to know him better.

Why?

He frowned up at the newly painted ceiling. Why was it important to him that Jenny meet his family, understand his background, his roots?

The answer slid into his mind almost casually, as if it had been waiting in the wings for him to finally address the question.

He was going to marry Jenny Lathrop. He'd known it on a gut level for some time now without consciously admitting it to himself. And though there were any number of horrific problems to be overcome—not the least of which was Jenny's indifference to having a husband—he'd give her time.

He heard her now, saying goodbye at last. "See you tomorrow afternoon, then. Night, Veronica."

Tomorrow afternoon? Tomorrow was Sunday. He'd planned on taking Jenny out on his sailboat.

She tiptoed into the room, thinking he was asleep. When she saw he wasn't, she made a flying leap at the bed, scurrying under the covers and pressing her icy body against his warmth.

"I'm frozen! It's cold out there. Veronica asked me to meet her for a cup of tea downtown tomorrow. She sounds desperately lonely. You don't mind, do you, Zach?"

He was methodically taking off the flannel nightgown, pulling his socks off her feet, warming her bare flesh with his hands and his body.

"Mind? Why should I mind? I'm going to have to spend the afternoon working on the Solomen case anyhow, so I'll probably miss dinner. The examination for discovery went ahead with no problems, and the trial is scheduled for the first week in November."

So he'd have a wife who spent Sundays having tea with bag ladies. He had no doubt Jenny would end up inviting Veronica or someone like her to their home for a good meal, if it came down to it.

What the hell. He'd learn to live with that.

A wicked grin came and went as he felt her beginning to melt under his conscientious stroking.

Maybe they'd invite his father over for one of those eclectic meals.

Zach had a feeling the unflappable Theodore Jones might have an exciting few years ahead of him, getting to really know the future mother of his grandchildren.

9

SHE WAS NICE AND WARM again. In fact, a few moments ago in his arms, she'd been scalding hot. And the lovemaking had made him forget the awkward discussion they'd been having about marriage.

She was thinking of the phone call. "Zach, you'll never believe what Veronica was telling me just now."

"Probably not, but try me anyway." His voice sounded sleepy. She ought to let him rest. Why was it lovemaking made her talkative and him tired?

"Well, she was going on about some guy she's having a relationship with. It sounds like all they do is fight. She's always telling me about her boyfriends. It's sad, because I'm certain most of it's her imagination. Anyhow, tonight she suddenly started telling me this story about being married once, a long time ago, to some singer named Conroy Clark. She got mad at me because I'd never heard of him. She said he's made several records, and that he's well-known around town. You know anybody by that name?"

Zach was nearly asleep; she could tell by the way his words slurred together. "Yeah. Sings blues, good guitarist. G'night, honey." He yawned, snuggled her closer, cupped one large, gentle hand around her right breast, and began to snore gently.

Jenny lay coiled in the security of his arms, thinking about Veronica. As usual, the older woman had been drinking when she phoned. Jenny felt deeply sorry for her.

She had similar feelings for many of her clients at the Legal Clinic—even though she'd learned that some told her outright lies about their predicaments.

It irritated her; it was a big waste of time when people were dishonest. It was disillusioning, as well. She'd never admit it to Zach, but her compassion was coupled now with skepticism. Her clients were definitely poor and underprivileged, but sometimes it wasn't surprising to see how they'd ended up that way. They had trouble making good decisions, and a number had the idea that life owed them—despite their lack of initiative.

She went over her visit today with Zach's family. They were the other side of the coin: filthy rich by Jenny's standards; privileged members of the upper class. If it weren't for the man asleep at her side, she'd never have put herself in a social situation like the one she'd weathered today. Attending an intimate family dinner at the Jones mansion on Marine Drive wasn't exactly high on her list of priorities. It had been an ordeal, and more than anything else, it pointed out to her the chasm that separated herself from Zach.

Not that his family hadn't been nice to her; Zach's sister, Serena, had even suggested they have lunch together one day soon. Jenny had said something noncommittal, vowing silently that it would be a chilly day in hell before she willingly ruined a lunch hour by choosing to spend it with Serena Jones.

She could feel the fuzziness of sleep creeping over her. Her last coherent thought was that this wonderful man—this magic interlude in her life—couldn't possibly last much longer.

ANOTHER WEEK PASSED. Seven hectic days of hard work and seven nights far too short for the lovemaking that filled them. The Solomen case was due to go to trial soon, and Zach was buried under a mountain of paperwork.

It was late afternoon on Tuesday, and he'd waded through most of it when Brenda buzzed.

"Mr. Solomen on line two, Mr. Jones."

Zach picked up the receiver. "David, how are you, I'm just—"

"Zach, the Safefood people are picketing me. They're all around this building." David's quiet voice was tense. "They're handing out leaflets and hollering slogans and doing their best to stop people from coming inside. They've got these big signs with skulls and crossbones all over them, and my customers have slowed to a trickle."

"Well, that does it. I'll get an injunction, get them stopped. I need to know how many protestors are there, exactly what they're saying, if they're physically blocking entry..."

He asked questions and made notes. "Sit tight, David. I'll be over there with an injunction as soon as I can."

He briefed Brenda on what was going on as he hurried out. She was extremely interested in the Solomen case, and she'd been remarkably helpful in its preparation, staying late and helping Zach prepare his statement of defense.

It took time—far more time than Zach expected—to obtain the injunction. Judge Paisley was old and cautious, and he questioned and reread every form twenty-three times before he finally agreed to sign. By the time Zach hurried out of the courthouse and into his car, it was rush hour.

The trip across town was endless. When Zach finally arrived at the block of stores that included Solomen's Organic Produce Mart, it was dusk, and he half expected the protestors would have packed up and gone home.

Instead, there seemed to be a riot going on in front of David's store. Several police cars were drawn up on the curb, red lights flashing, and a large, noisy crowd had gathered on the periphery of the action.

Zach shouldered his way through—official document safe in his briefcase, and a sense of foreboding growing in his stomach as the angry voices of the crowd grew louder.

As he drew near, he could see that the large front window of Solomen's store had been shattered, and the bins under the awning that had held fruits and vegetables were overturned. Oranges, lettuce and grapefruits were scattered everywhere.

A mobile TV-news truck was on hand, as well as several reporters.

"Who's in charge here? I'm Mr. Solomen's lawyer and I have a court order barring these people from any further picketing." The young officer Zach questioned pointed toward a police car where another officer was standing. Zach walked over and explained to the burly sergeant about the court order, and then demanded, "What happened here?"

The sergeant shook his head. "Started out with just
these protestors, but then a lady came along, real feisty,
started telling them what to do with their signs, and the
big tall guy over there, name of Paul Jensen, he hassled
her, calling her a few names and crowding her some.
He's the organizer of this whole thing. Anyhow, Solomen came charging out of the store and socked the guy
a good one. They had a battle over there on the sidewalk, and the other protestors went right out of control."

The sergeant shook his head in disgust. "Somebody
in the crowd threw a chunk of cement through the window, smashed it to smithereens, somebody else turned
over the bins, the lady got in the act and kicked one of
the protestors a good one. Don't usually see this kind
of violence over somethin' like this. More often it's a
strike where this happens. Never thought vegetarians
were the violent sort. Anyhow, you got a court order,
that's Paul Jensen over there you serve, the big guy with
the bruise on his face and the bleeding nose. I'll just tail
along, be sure he pays attention."

"Where's my client now? Mr. Solomen?" Zach half
expected to hear that David had been taken to hospital.

"Inside the store, with the lady. This yo-yo Jensen's
screamin' about pressin' charges, but with the window
broken and all, I figure he's on thin ice there."

With the officer standing behind him, Zach read the
court order and handed it to the sullen Jensen.

The officer, with the help of a loud-hailer, informed
the protestors that either they disappeared or they faced
arrest, and within minutes the area was cleared. Only

the television people with their mobile cameras were left on the scene, and they came hurrying over to Zach.

"I understand you're Mr. Solomen's lawyer. Can you tell us what's going on here?"

As clearly and concisely as he could, Zach told a young woman reporter about the picketing and the injunction, avoiding any judgmental comments.

"Can you tell us more about the impending court case against Mr. Solomen? We understand he's selling contaminated produce...."

Zach walked away without further comment. A frightened young clerk unlocked the front door and let him into the store, and Zach headed up the stairs at the back to where he knew David's office was.

He opened the door, and found David Solomen with his arms around a curvaceous blond woman. They were kissing—a passionate kiss that broke off reluctantly when Zach cleared his throat. "Sorry to interrupt, but I need to know exactly what happened out there."

They turned toward him, and Zach could hardly believe his eyes.

The woman in David's arms was Brenda Pennington, and she had the beginnings of a spectacular black eye.

STILL GLEEFULLY PLANNING the conversation he would have with Brenda the following morning at the office, Zach drove to Jenny's. She'd offered to cook him dinner tonight, and he was good and late, but she'd understand when he explained what had happened.

He glanced at his watch. Damn, it was almost nine. He'd tried to phone from David's store, but there was no answer at the apartment, which bothered him a little.

Where was Jenny, anyhow?

The basement door was unlocked. Zach hurried in. The apartment was empty, but there was the smell of onions cooking, and a pot of potatoes by the sink. A bowl of apples, half peeled, lay abandoned on the table beside the phone. There was also a note.

Veronica in trouble. Gone to city jail to rescue her. Can you pick me up at her house, 4905 Powell? Will wait for you there.

J.

Feeling as if he'd taken up permanent residence in his car, Zach drove downtown. Veronica's address was in a rough area. Zach parked the car under a streetlamp and locked it. A gang of young toughs on the corner eyed the sports car and made remarks about Zach's suit. An old man staggered by, so drunk he was barely able to stay upright.

Feeling edgy, Zach hurried along the sidewalk, trying to read the numbers on the run-down buildings. The houses here were close together, their front doors only a few feet from the crumbling sidewalk. Most of them were in darkness. Halfway down the street, Zach found 4905 and stumbled his way up the rotting front steps to ring the bell.

There was no answer. There wasn't any light at the front of the house, either. He tried again and decided the bell wasn't working. The front door was locked.

What the hell was going on here, and where was Jenny?

There was a faint light and the muted sound of voices coming from the back, so he fumbled his way around the side of the house, muttering curses under his breath, when he tripped on something and almost fell.

There was a small porch with two steps. The door was half glass, and just before Zach raised his hand to knock he looked inside. His hand dropped.

The tableau was lit harshly by a naked bulb that dangled at the end of a cord hanging from the kitchen ceiling. Jenny was backed against a cupboard, and there was fear in her eyes. Veronica, with one arm doubled up behind her back, was being held by a short man with a huge stomach. His face was a deep bloodred, and Zach could hear Veronica's hysterical voice through the door.

"Nobody uses me for a mud slide! Get your filthy hands off me, Louie—"

Zach took a deep breath, gripped the doorknob, twisted, and threw it open violently. It smashed back and into the wall.

As loudly and forcefully as he could, Zach bellowed, "What's going on in here? Take your hands off that woman! What d'you think you're doing? Move away, just move away. . . ."

Keeping up a steady stream of commands, he swiftly placed himself between the man and Jenny, watching for a knife or gun and feeling the adrenaline course through his veins. If the guy had a weapon, this could get ugly fast.

Veronica screamed at the top of her lungs when he burst in—a shocking, high-pitched siren of sound—and the man hollered, "Holy Jesus! It's the cops!" He dropped Veronica's arm and whirled so he was facing Zach.

Veronica immediately turned to the cupboard, picked up a plate, and smashed it over his bald head. He let out a roar of pain, and pieces of crockery flew everywhere. A bright spot of blood appeared on his shiny skull, and he reached a hand up to check for damages, staring at the blood in horror.

"Jesus, woman, you cut me! What the hell—"

"Asshole! Liar! Cheat!" Without a pause, Veronica grabbed a pot from the sink, full of oily water, and tossed it over the man, then raised the pot to hit him with it.

Greasy water dripping off his head and shirt, he raised his arms to protect himself, backing toward the door. "Whatsa matter with you? You crazy or somethin'? You're crazy, y'hear me?"

Veronica advanced, hollering, "Get out, you creep! I never want to see you again!"

The man reached the doorway, threw himself out and raced into the darkness. Veronica slammed the door behind him and locked it.

There was a moment of silence in the kitchen. Zach could feel the tension in his muscles gradually begin to ease. He turned toward Jenny and she collapsed in his arms. He could feel her body trembling.

"God, Zach, I've never been so glad to see anybody."

Zach held her tightly, aware as never before how fragile her body felt against his. He looked over her head at Veronica, who was now taking off several of her coats, although her red toque was still pulled down over her ears. She was muttering to herself under her breath.

"What the hell is going on here, Jenny? Mrs. Glickman, where's your phone? I'm calling the police."

Veronica looked at him as if he were demented. "What for?" she queried, using one foot to gather the pieces of glass into a careless pile. "That's just Louie. He figured he could stay here but I kicked him out. He won't be back. Anyhow, I don't have a phone. Wouldn't want to get Louie in trouble even if I had. I know that creep. He's just a coward. There's no point in getting the police involved." Her face drew into an angry grimace. "Two-timin' little snot, I oughta broke his head for him good." She moved around the kitchen, opening the oven door and taking out a kettle. "Lucky thing I can take care of myself. You and me both can. Right, Miss Jenny? You want some tea? Or maybe a drink. I know there's some rye around here somewhere, 'less that sponger drank it...." Muttering to herself, she began opening cupboard doors and poking in drawers.

Zach unhooked Jenny's arms from their death clasp on his rib cage and held her away from him. Her face was pale, every freckle standing out in bold relief.

"Jenny, will you tell me what the hell this is all about? What are you doing down here in the first place?"

Her glasses were crooked and she reached up and straightened them. She looked embarrassed as she explained.

"Veronica phoned a couple of hours ago from the city jail. She'd been picked up for causing a disturbance in a bar, and she was pretty upset. I only had money for taxi fare one way, so that's why I left you that note. Anyhow, they released her on my recognizance and we walked over here. That man, Louie, was here in the kitchen, waiting. It was him Veronica had the fight with in the bar. She says he's been living with her, and she caught him tonight with another woman, and she lost her temper. He seemed violent. I didn't know for sure what he'd do next, and each time I tried to get out the door to go for help, he came at me." She shuddered. "There's no phone, and I wasn't sure any of the neighbors would come and help, anyhow. It's a pretty strange neighborhood. I was really scared," she confessed in a small voice.

Zach could feel his tension turning to horror as he imagined all the atrocities that might have occurred. "Let's get the hell out of here."

Jenny nodded. Veronica was still searching aimlessly through cupboards, and Jenny went over to her and took her arm to get her attention. "Veronica, we're going now. You stay inside and keep the doors locked tonight. No more brawling in bars, either. You understand?"

Veronica nodded cheerfully. "You got a smoke? I'm clean out of cigarettes."

Jenny sighed. "You know I don't smoke. Now, you heard what I told you? No going out—not for cigarettes or anything else. If the police see you wandering around again tonight, they'll haul you in. You heard what they said. I promised them I'd bring you straight home and you'd stay here."

"And I will." Veronica sounded insulted. "I'm a woman of my word, you know that, Miss Jenny." She gave Zach a long, measuring look. "Don't I know you? Weren't you the one got smacked that night at the Legal Clinic? Good thing you had a smart lady to rescue you that time, huh?"

Zach didn't answer. He was doing his best to keep his temper in check, but it was a losing battle. He was tired, and he was hungry. He wanted nothing more than to get Jenny and himself out of here and he didn't need any smart-mouthing from Veronica. The past few hours had been far too full of tension, and he still wasn't sure they were out of the woods.

"C'mon." He took Jenny firmly by the arm and led her through the dark house to the front door, aware of the sweet, sickly smell of years of neglect that permeated the place. He stumbled over various pieces of furniture and random boxes of junk as he went.

He fumbled with the chain lock and opened the front door. He looked carefully up and down the street before he led Jenny down the steps to the sidewalk, hustling her along to where he'd parked his car, grateful that Louie seemed to have vanished. So had everyone else. The dingy street was deserted.

About to unlock the passenger door, he stared in horror at an inch-wide gouge etched into his paint job, stretching from the back bumper to the front fender. There was an identical scratch on the driver's side.

He looked up and down the street for whoever was responsible, but there wasn't a single person in sight. Even the gang on the corner had disappeared.

A slow rage began to build inside him. He climbed in and slammed the door, thrust the key in the ignition and as soon as the motor caught, roared away, his jaw clenched.

"Zach?" Jenny's voice was uncertain. "I'm sorry about the car."

He made a superhuman effort at controlling his anger and failed. Furious words—words of anger compounded by frustration and fear for her safety—spilled out.

"It's not just the damned car, Jenny. I can have the car repainted. All I can think of is what might have happened to you back there. Do you have any idea how it makes me feel, having you wandering around this area alone at night, ending up in situations like that one? What if I hadn't made it down here when I did?"

She was immediately defensive. "But Veronica's my client. I can't very well just ignore a call from her when she needs me, can I?"

Zach tried to curb his anger, tried to inject some reason into his tone. "Jenny, it wouldn't hurt to let her sit it out in jail for a couple of hours, to wait until I could go with you."

She immediately got huffy. "Veronica can't stand being locked up. She goes crazy. She has this phobia. Besides, I don't need a chaperon, Zach. I'm a grown woman. I'm a lawyer—or I will be in a few months."

What was left of his control snapped. "You've got a hell of a lot to learn before you call yourself a lawyer! You fall for every cock-and-bull, down-and-out story you're handed. You let yourself get sucked into downright dangerous situations like this one tonight."

"For heaven's sake, Zach, I made an error in judgment. Don't you ever make mistakes?"

"Not with clients. I do my homework. I don't fall for every sob story I hear. I check out the facts." He could hear himself, sounding as righteous as a television evangelist, and couldn't seem to stop. This whole thing had gone too far. Things that had been sore points for weeks were close to the surface now, ready to erupt like boils. His voice was thick with disgust. "People like

Veronica and that . . . Louie . . . Damn it, Jenny! You go on believing they're victims, when it's really *you* who's the scapegoat in the whole thing. You don't even get paid for putting your life on the line this way, for God's sake."

As soon as he said it, he knew it was the wrong, the very worst thing he could say. His mouth just seemed to have clicked into automatic.

"So, really, you're furious with me because I don't get a nice fat fee for what I'm doing. Isn't that right?" Her voice was trembling. "With you, it always comes down to money in the end, doesn't it? This much time and effort and concern equals this much money. To hell with the human factor."

"Don't be ridiculous. Money has nothing to do with this, and you know it."

"Oh, but it has everything to do with it! If Veronica were rich, you'd probably take her on as a client yourself, eccentric or not. If—" her voice was going out of control, and he was sorry he'd ever started all this "—if Elias Redthorn had money, he'd at least have some compensation for having to wear that body brace the rest of his life."

Zach slammed a hand down on the steering wheel. "How in God's name did Elias bloody Redthorn get into this? Would you tell me that?"

She gulped and went straight on. "Because if he had money, your precious firm would have taken his case. If..." She sniffed hard and scrabbled through her purse for a tissue, without success.

Zach found one in his pocket and handed it to her, and she blew her nose hard. He knew exactly where this

was heading, and he didn't want to hear about it tonight.

Before she could say anything, he heard himself
snarl, "And I'm sick to death of hearing about how you
and those other poor women were taken advantage of
by big bad business lawyers when your husband was
killed, so don't bother telling me all over again."

Even as he said it, he knew why. He was a jealous
fool, and he didn't want to be reminded she'd had a
husband she cared about.

"Stop this car right now." Her hand was on the latch,
and she had the door open.

"Jesus, Jenny—"

He reached for her arm with one hand and pulled
sharply to the curb with the other.

Jenny pried his hand off her arm and slid out. "If
you're that tired of hearing what I have to say, then you
don't have to listen anymore, because I never want to
see you again, Zachary Jones." She slammed the door
hard enough to wreck the hinges.

"Jenny, get back in this car—"

A bus pulled up beside him and the driver leaned on
the horn, glaring down at him. He was in a bus zone.
Zach cursed and pulled out, watching for a parking
spot. He found one just in time to see Jenny get on the
bus.

Fuming, he pulled out into traffic and stepped fero-
ciously on the gas. He'd wait for her at her place, and
they'd get this straightened out, once and for all. He was
zigzagging at a reckless speed through traffic on
Broadway when he heard the siren.

The policeman asked if he'd been drinking, then gave
him a lecture and a sizable ticket. When the patrol car

pulled away at last, Zach sat for a minute or two, breathing slowly in and out. This wasn't his night.

Carefully, he started his engine and drove to his apartment. There were times when a temporary retreat was in order, and this was one of them.

He had a full bottle of Scotch in the cupboard over the refrigerator, and he broke the seal and poured himself a water glass full, with two ice cubes, before he dialed Jenny's number.

The line was busy.

He spent the next three hours alternately waiting for Jenny to phone him, trying to call her, and drinking whiskey.

Each time he dialed, the line was busy.

He finally realized she'd unplugged the phone, and that enraged him so much he had two more drinks.

He'd go over and have this out with her first thing in the morning, by God. *Before* he went to work.

He fell asleep on the couch at quarter past three.

10

BRENDA CALLED the apartment at nine forty-five the next morning, dragging Zach out of a drugged sleep and into a world of pain.

After twenty rings, he finally managed to find the telephone, aware only that he was in agony. His head had been invaded by demons, his stomach was churning, and it was beginning to dawn on him that he'd had a serious disagreement with Jenny.

He lifted the receiver and managed to indicate that he was still alive. Barely.

"Mr. Jones, the investigator, Mr. King, is here. You had an appointment with him this morning to go over the reports on the Solomen case. And you have to file the Pattison documents with the court registrar at one. And then you have appointments with two clients, one of them is Mr. Tremone from Hart, Mason and Stewart. And, Mr. Jones?"

Zach cleared his throat and managed a hoarse, "Yes, Brenda?"

"I really need to talk to you, too, Mr. Jones." It was the first time in over four years he'd ever heard her sound vulnerable.

"How's that shiner this morning, Brenda?" He'd had a whole list of smart remarks to tease her with, but his own misery made them seem cruel. Pain was a great leveler.

"Awful. I'm wearing dark glasses, but I'm still liable to scare away clients." The words were meant to be an attempt at humor, but her voice quavered. "And there're pictures in the morning paper, and Mr. Meredith and Mr. Hanover saw the whole episode on the late news last night. They said your tie was crooked. They've been quite vocal about my eye, as well."

Zach just bet they were vocal. Brenda had given them all enough tongue-lashings over the years about their own escapades to make this seem a golden opportunity for getting even.

He couldn't really blame them; he'd been planning something of the sort himself last night.

"Never mind them, Brenda. They're green with jealousy, seeing you with David Solomen. Look, take it easy. I'll be in as soon as I can. Ask Ozzie if he can wait half an hour. Knowing him, he'll bill me for the time anyway."

The moment the phone was free, he dialed Jenny's number.

It rang fourteen times before he hung up. Obviously, she'd already left for classes.

It took heavy-duty pain-relief capsules and a boiling-hot shower to enable him to get as far as the office.

A genuinely subdued and bruised Brenda took one look at him and poured him a giant mug of freshly brewed black coffee.

"You look dreadful, Mr. Jones." She sounded truly concerned.

He squinted at the oversize dark glasses she wore and the pallor of her face under the careful application of makeup.

"Well, you don't look half bad, Brenda," he managed to lie gallantly. "Women must be tougher than men."

When it came right down to it, there was a lot of compensation to having a Brenda Pennington with a few human problems. Any other time, she'd have tormented him with righteous remarks about alcoholism and taken delight in feeding him lukewarm instant coffee.

"Mr. King is waiting up in your office."

Zach took two long swallows from his mug and struggled up the stairs.

"Mornin', young man." Investigator Ozzie King was in fine form, suit as rumpled as ever, bloodshot beagle eyes quick to take in Zach's condition. "Tied on a good one, did ya? Happens to the best of us, counselor. I brought in these surveillance reports." He gestured to an enormous stack of paper on Zach's desk. "I'll go over them with ya now. There's a few details I need to explain."

It took eons. Ozzie left nothing out—which was why the firm used him—but his insistence on covering every last bruise on every last grapefruit meant that Zach had to swallow two more painkillers and then skip lunch in order to get rid of Ozzie and still arrive at the registrar's office at one. When he was finished there, he tried to get hold of Jenny by calling the law faculty at UBC, but after an interminable wait he was told she couldn't be located.

He dragged himself back to the office and found Brenda waiting anxiously for him.

"I really need to talk with you, Mr. Jones. It's urgent." She looked as bad as it was possible for a ravishing blonde to look, which Zach figured was about one millionth as bad as he looked right about now.

"Unless we do it over some lunch, Brenda, it's going to have to wait until tomorrow. I haven't had anything to eat yet today, and I'm about to collapse. How long have we got before my next appointment?"

She consulted the diary. "Exactly forty-five minutes. But Mr. Tremone is usually about ten minutes late."

"Let's go."

Brenda's ironclad policy had always been not to accept so much as a ride from any of the partners. It was unfortunate that both Ken and Derek saw them leave the building and get into Zach's car, but their raised eyebrows, wolf whistles and smart remarks were way down on the list of things Zach felt like getting concerned about today.

He chose a restaurant nearby. The waitress brought him a steaming bowl of chicken soup to start, and Brenda ordered a large salad and herbal tea. "I've been a vegetarian for years," she explained when Zach urged her to join him in having a steak.

In four years of working with her every day, Zach hadn't known that. There were probably lots of things about Brenda he didn't know, and the thing was, now that he had Jenny, he wasn't even mildly curious. A few months ago, talking Brenda into having lunch with him would have been a major coup. Today, all he could think about was Jenny and the quarrel they'd had.

A feeling of depression overwhelmed him.

Brenda considerately waited until he was almost done spooning up the broth before she began.

"I wanted to talk to you about David Solomen," she said at last, and her lovely skin flushed a dusky rose beneath the dark glasses still hiding her eyes. She fidgeted with her cutlery and refolded the napkin she hadn't used.

"Now, why isn't that a surprise?" Zach was trying to make her smile, but it was hopeless. "You're in love with him, right?" he added in a much gentler tone. He knew all about being in love. It could hurt like hell.

"Yes, I am. He's—" Brenda flushed "—he's everything I ever wanted in a man. But we have problems that I need to discuss with you. There are things he hasn't told you."

Zach's stomach gurgled. "Omigod. He's contaminating his own vegetables? He's paying somebody off to do it? The whole case is a big fraud?"

He was only half joking. Today he had the feeling that anything was possible—as long as it was bad.

"Please, Mr. Jones, don't tease at a time like this." Brenda was visibly upset. "David is the most honorable man I've ever met. He would never do anything like that."

"Thank the powers that be for minor blessings." Zach slouched back in his seat. There was a limit today to how much he could deal with calmly.

The waitress arrived with his steak and Brenda's salad.

"You really shouldn't load your system with dead flesh, plus all that dairy," she admonished when he began loading on sour cream, chives and five packages of butter into his baked potato. "It clogs your arteries. You're not all that young anymore, Mr. Jones. If you must have the steak, you ought to just have salad with it. You shouldn't mix protein with heavy carbohy-drates."

He gave her a long look, and she blushed and then kept quiet about his eating habits.

When he'd devoured a fair portion of his food, she blurted, "First of all, I wanted to thank you for taking David's case on contingency. I know you had a hard time getting Mr. Meredith and Mr. Hanover to agree. David was probably too proud to tell you why he doesn't have any money. Am I right?"

"He didn't go into detail, no." Zach took another bite of the steak. The food was gradually easing the sickness in his stomach, and he felt more alive than he had all day. He'd try Jenny at home in an hour or so. She'd be finished classes early today. He'd pick her up and maybe they'd go to his place. They could make up on his water bed.... He forced himself to pay attention to what Brenda was saying.

"A lot of David's profits go to helping support his younger brother Melvin and Melvin's family, you see. David and Melvin were partners in the produce busi-ness, but Melvin was badly hurt in a car accident two years ago. He can't work, and he needs expensive ther-apy if he's ever to walk again. The insurance company found him not at fault for the accident, but there wasn't any settlement because the other guy was driving an out-of-province car with no insurance."

Zach now had a premonition of what was coming, and his heart sank. Why was this happening to him over and over again? First Jenny, now Brenda. First Redthorn, now Melvin Solomen. He began to eat his baked potato, listening to the rest of the story, know-ing what Brenda was going to ask him to do. Being

Brenda, she was as thorough as possible about setting him up.

"See, Melvin has three kids—three young boys—and David is making sure they get things like hockey equipment and football uniforms. He makes certain Melvin has the equipment and care he needs for rehabilitation. It costs a lot of money. David has all his own expenses, as well. When the stores are doing well, he just manages to make ends meet."

She fidgeted with her sunglasses and then took them off. Her eye was swollen, but she'd done a good job of masking it with makeup.

"I've offered to help. I've got some money from a few investments I've made, but David won't hear of it. And neither will he agree to getting married." She met Zach's gaze with a forlorn look. "He feels the financial pressure would eventually cause us problems. And maybe he's right. But the truth is, I'm not getting any younger myself, Mr. Jones. And now that I've found the man I want, I'd like to get married and get started on a family of my own."

Did David Solomen know what he was getting into here? But then he looked at her face, and felt rotten for thinking that way.

Tears were slowly trickling down her cheeks. She sniffed and took a deep breath, dabbing at her eyes with a napkin. "Mr. Jones, I know it's asking a lot, but could you look at the circumstances surrounding Melvin's case and maybe do something about it? They've had some guy from Legal Aid supposedly working on it, but he hasn't made any headway. They need a high-powered lawyer like you, Mr. Jones, if they're ever going to get anywhere. Oh, Mr. Jones, it would mean so much to me."

And what would it mean to Zach? She didn't say so, but of course the case would be *pro bono*. He thought of the money the firm had already spent on Solomen—the investigative charges, the time invested in preparing a statement of defense, the hours and hours spent going over evidence; and it was going to take at least another two days in court when the case was heard.

The fees were on contingency, and if he lost, the firm would be out a sizable amount of money. And there were no guarantees this new problem would result in a positive verdict, either. Even if it did, he'd never bill for his services. Not under the circumstances.

He ought to simply say no to Brenda. A few months ago, he'd have done just that without any qualms; he'd have hidden behind the firm's policies, his partners' decisions, his own hardheaded assumptions about business.

That was before Jenny. The story Brenda told was all too reminiscent of Jenny, of the situations she described both from her own life and from the lives of people at the legal-aid clinic.

Jenny had changed him—changed the way he reacted to people. A few months ago, he'd have considered what Brenda had just told him unfortunate, but not a deciding influence in his business dealings with Solomen. Hell, if it hadn't been for Jenny, he probably wouldn't be dealing with Solomen at all.

Because of Jenny, he'd been forced to see people differently than he had before—as individuals with circumstances and destinies less fortunate than his.

Destinies he might have the ability to change, if he cared to.

He could hear Jenny's voice clearly, accusing him of basing his decisions solely on whether or not people could pay a nice fat fee.

Still . . . "If I were the only one involved, I wouldn't hesitate to take on Melvin's case," he began slowly. "The problem is, just as you said, Ken and Derek weren't happy about taking the Solomen case on at all, and I have to consider their reactions to a second one."

Brenda bristled. "The publicity the firm got last night should be worth something in itself, shouldn't it, Mr. Jones? We could remind Mr. Meredith and Mr. Hanover that publicity is worth money."

"It wasn't altogether positive publicity, Brenda." Zach tried to be gentle, but there was no escaping the fact that the papers had blown her role completely out of context, and emphasized her connection with the firm defending Solomen in a derisive sort of way. Paul Jensen was clever at manipulating the press, all right. Zach figured he was using the case as a publicity stunt, just as David had said he might.

Which definitely put David in the role of innocent victim.

"Look, Brenda, let me get this case of David's out of the way, and then I promise I'll give this other thing serious consideration."

Even if he didn't take Melvin's case through the firm, the least he could do would be to review the facts and make some recommendations. Hell, he could get Jenny involved. She'd love working on something like this, and she'd never give up until they won a settlement for

Melvin, either. His spirits rose at the thought of working with her on it.

Brenda leaned across and put her hand on his, giving it a grateful squeeze. "I don't know how to thank you, Mr. Jones."

"There's one thing you could do, Brenda."

"What's that?"

"You could please for the love of God start calling me Zach."

THEY HURRIED BACK to the office, and Mr. Tremone was waiting, not pleased at all about the delay.

Somehow, Zach made it through the rest of the afternoon. When his last client finally left, he drove to Jenny's, using every shortcut he knew. A sense of urgency had been building in him all afternoon—a desperate need to see her, to smooth away the harsh words and anger of the night before.

He knocked, and she opened the door. She didn't rush into his embrace as he'd half hoped she might, and his heart sank. It would be easy, if only he could touch her, hold her. When she was in his arms, they never fought.

"Hello, Zach. Come in." She sounded remote and cool. This was going to be tough.

She looked pale and drawn—her bright hair a startling flash of color against her skin. Her blue eyes were tired-looking behind her glasses, and he felt remorse. She'd probably not slept well, and it was partly his fault.

"Jenny, I . . ." he began, but she interrupted, holding a hand up toward him, palm out, warding him off and talking quickly in a flat tone of voice, as if she'd prepared an unpleasant speech and was determined to deliver it.

"I've been doing a lot of thinking since last night, Zach, and this isn't going to work between us at all. What happened is bound to happen again—our beliefs and ideals about the law are too different. *We're* too different," she added with such a note of sadness in her voice that he longed to take the three steps that separated them, sweep her into his arms, and use his mouth to smother the things she was saying.

"I think it's better if we stop seeing each other. Permanently."

"Jenny..."

What was she saying? He took two steps toward her, and she moved away. There was an aloofness about her that infuriated him—an invisible barrier she'd put up between them. Her words registered, but he couldn't believe she meant them. He wanted to pull her into his arms, take her to the bedroom, grind his flesh into hers and make her cry out, hot and sweet and eager for his loving, the way she had so many times before.

"Jenny, that's ridiculous. So we had a disagreement. That's not the end of the world. Everybody has them. Surely we can talk it out."

Her eyes were unrelenting. "We *have* talked. As far as I'm concerned, there's nothing more to say."

But there was. He needed to tell her that he loved her, that the thought of not seeing her again was intolerable to him.

"I can't respect someone who puts money ahead of everything else," she said in a cool tone. "I can't respect someone who won't fight for the underdog without first thinking about a fee."

The unfairness of the accusation hit him like a punch in the gut. Pride kept him from defending himself. "Is that truly what you believe about me, Jenny?"

She stared at him for a long moment, and then she shrugged.

"What else can I believe? You've never given me any reason to think otherwise."

Before he could say anything else, she walked to the door, skirting around him carefully so she wouldn't touch him. She opened it and stood there.

"I think you'd better go now," she said in a stony voice, not meeting his eyes.

He thought of all the denials he could make, and then he thought about all the arguments they'd already gone through. Words weren't going to solve this. He'd tried that.

He considered taking her in his arms and using his lips and hands and body to change her mind. He knew if he did, it would work for right now. The sensual bond between them was overwhelming. But the time would inevitably come when the whole issue reared its head all over again.

Somehow, he had to find a way to convince her, once and for all, that she was wrong about his motives. It hurt—her assessment of him.

It was going to take time, and right now he was far too weary and heartsick and hung over to figure out a way. And her words were making him angry all over again.

"If that's how you really feel, I think you're right. I will go. Goodbye, Jenny."

HOURS LATER, curled in a miserable heap on her bed, she finally ran out of tears. She'd known all along it had to end; it was better to get it over with now, wasn't it? Before . . . before what? some remorseless voice interrupted.

Before she'd fallen hopelessly in love with him?

What a joke that was.

GOING TO THE LEGAL clinic the next night took every scrap of courage she possessed, but she needn't have been worried about it, because Zach didn't attend. An older lawyer, Mr. Humphreys, was there instead, and Jenny overhead one of the students asking him where Mr. Jones was.

"He won't be able to make it for a couple of weeks. He's tied up with a case that's taking all his time," Humphreys said.

Jenny felt a mixture of relief and wretched disappointment.

Some part of her had been hoping, in spite of everything, that Zach would be there.

And then what? He'd beg her to forgive him, she'd fall into his arms, and everything would be perfect forever?

Get real, Lathrop. Let him go. Don't humiliate yourself by chasing after what was only a dream.

But as day followed day, Jenny struggled with the almost-overwhelming urge to phone him, to grovel, to make any compromises with her conscience just to be able to be with him.

Like a blow to the chest that never stopped hurting, she came to understood at last the full extent of her feelings for Zach.

She loved him. In her entire life, she'd never loved a man this way; never loved any person with this degree of intensity. Every pore, every inch of her body, every sense longed for him, for the feel of his arms, the smell of his skin, the sound of his voice. When Nick was killed, she'd grieved for him, but not like this; not with this all-consuming physical and mental anguish. At times, she literally felt she'd die without him.

She couldn't sleep well. At first, food held no interest, and then she began to eat all the time, as if by filling her stomach, she'd fill the emptiness that losing him had left inside of her.

She was short-tempered with her clients at the Legal Clinic.

Ironically, now that Zach wasn't around to point it out, she could see clearly that for some of them the choices they'd made led directly to their problems. The more she became involved in their lives, the less she believed in an indifferent fate that penalized one person and allowed another to go free.

She began to see some of the self-destructive ways in which they created their own destiny.

Veronica was a case in point.

The second Thursday without Zach—which was how Jenny had begun to measure the days—Veronica was waiting for Jenny at the Legal Clinic just as she always was.

She didn't usually need legal advice; she considered Jenny her friend, and the clinic a social gathering.

"Hi, Miss Jenny. I brought you a doughnut for coffee break."

Jenny accepted the offering, wanly smiling her thanks, conscious as always of the pungent, moldy smell that emanated from Veronica's layers of clothing. Tonight she had at least four coats on, with the longest under the others. Crooked hemlines hung one below the other, one green, one dark brown, one beige, and the top one, black. She'd taken off her woolen toque, and her scarecrow hair stood up as if she'd suffered an electric shock. The inevitable cigarette dangled from one hand, unlit because the clinic was a nonsmoking area.

Jenny wearily took her place behind her rickety table. She wondered how she was going to dispose of the doughnut without Veronica noticing. Small issues grew monumental now, and it seemed that life would never be full of laughter or wonder or joy again.

"Long and straight and dusty to the grave." Now, where had she read that? It certainly described her life without Zach.

Her first client, a lanky middle-aged man, ambled over and sat down. Jenny began the ritual of the waiver.

She glanced up from filling in the man's name and groaned aloud. Veronica had evaded the volunteer and was standing over Jenny's client, scowling down at him.

"No point even talkin' to him, honey," she announced in her rough voice, thrusting a finger under the man's nose. "He's nothin' but a con man. I know for a fact he gets Welfare under two different names. Probably wants you to figure out how he can set up a third, if I know him. You don't want to bother with the likes of that."

Naturally, Jenny's client objected to this, and it led to a loud argument between him and Veronica. Mr. Humphreys came hurrying over, and in a few moments, Veronica and the man were both assisted out the door, still shouting at one another.

Humphreys gave Jenny a mild lecture filled with advice about dealing with clients with mental problems, and Jenny was too despondent to even argue.

Veronica did have mental problems, and the truth was she was becoming a major nuisance.

Late that night, Jenny had just fallen into an exhausted doze when the phone rang. Heart thumping, knowing it couldn't be Zach but praying anyway, Jenny tumbled out of bed, ran blindly into the other room and picked up the receiver.

"Miss Jenny? Miss Jenny, I'm sorry for what happened tonight, but I was right. That man . . ."

Bitterly disappointed, tired to the bone, Jenny lost her patience and gave Veronica a tongue-lashing, adding that she didn't want Veronica phoning her at home again unless it was a true emergency.

Veronica started to cry, and Jenny felt like a heel. "I was just tryin' to help you out, one woman to another. I'm no bag lady, y'know," Veronica sniffled in her ear. "I got pride, I got friends, I got a house of my own. I don't hafta stay down here if I don't want to. I could sell for a bundle any time I like. And if I snap my fingers, old Conroy'll come back to me, too. See if he don't. He's playing at the Bayshore this week. You and that fancy boyfriend ought to go hear him. Conroy Clark's really somethin' to hear."

Jenny lost her temper all over again. "Veronica, that's all your imagination and you know it is. Now, get a grip on reality here. If you start bothering this Clark man, you're going to end up in jail, you hear me? And I won't be able to do a darned thing about it, either, so you—"

Veronica hung up in Jenny's ear.

To FINISH a homework assignment a few days later, Jenny had to search a property claim at the Land Registry Office. When she had the information she needed, she looked up the tax information on Veronica's house, suspecting that her batty client was probably in serious arrears; but the taxes were paid up to date, always before they were due, always by check.

Payment was made—had been made for years—by a Mr. Conroy Clark.

SOMEONE WHO PUTS money ahead of all else.

Someone who won't fight for the underdog without first considering the fee.

Jenny's parting words had sliced into Zach like knife wounds. For the first few days, he felt lacerated, sliced open by her opinion of him, mortally wounded by the woman he loved.

Then he took refuge in cold, bitter anger. How could she believe he was heartless? How dare she accuse him of being a money-grubbing, selfish person? Didn't she know him better than that by now? He worked himself into a fury and told himself he was well rid of her.

At work, he was dangerously short-tempered. Ken and Derek began to avoid him.

Brenda couldn't. And one morning, after he'd snapped at her over the intercom again for very little reason, Zach looked up from some documents he couldn't make sense of to find her in his office.

He scowled. "What is it, Brenda? Surely you can see I'm busy."

Her bruised eye had healed, and she was giving him a look that might have made lesser men shiver in their Italian loafers.

"Look here, Mr—Zach." She shoved the door shut behind her and advanced toward his desk. "I'm sick and tired of having you suffer in silence and take out your foul temper on me." She plumped herself down in the leather client's chair and crossed her legs, causing her leather miniskirt to ride dangerously high on her thighs.

Zach didn't even notice.

"I came to you when I needed someone to talk to. Surely you could do the same with me. Your lady's dumped you, right?"

Zach gave her a look that ought to have shut her up forever, but Brenda was entirely unaffected. "Don't forget, Zachary, I've come to know you rather well in the years I've worked here. You've been foul-tempered before, but it's never lasted this long, and you've never been quite this . . . mean." She gave him a level look. "Are you in love with this Jenny Lathrop? You've certainly changed since you've been seeing her, and I had thought for the better."

There wasn't much point in asking how Brenda knew about Jenny, or how much she knew. Zach figured she probably had meticulous files on every woman the three partners had dated for the past four years. He wondered for a moment if Interpol had any inkling what they'd slipped up on by not hiring Brenda Pennington.

He considered ordering her out of his office, but the anger that had sustained him for days was wearing thin enough to allow for a semblance of clear thinking.

What came through was the truth.

He slumped down in his chair and closed his eyes. Images of a redheaded vixen was there, waiting to taunt him.

"Yeah, I do. I do love Jenny Lathrop." It felt good to admit it.

"And she *has* dumped you?"

"For God's sake, Brenda, why don't you mind your own..." Zach glared at her.

Brenda didn't even blink.

Zach slumped again and sighed. "Yeah, she has. Irreconcilable differences having arisen, and all that."

Brenda stood and brushed her skirt into place with the air of someone who'd gotten to the root of a problem. "Well, then, Zachary, instead of acting like a bear with a sore head, I suggest you apply your fine mind to getting her back. You are a lawyer, after all. Lawyers are supposed to be good at logic, aren't they?"

She marched out.

Zach abandoned the file folders and did what Brenda had suggested. By noon, he'd arrived at several conclusions.

The first was that in spite of everything—and there was a lot of everything to consider here; it was Jenny he was dealing with—he loved her passionately, and he wasn't about to lose her. In fact, he was going to marry her, even if he had to carry her kicking and screaming to the altar.

That decision consoled him momentarily, and he considered ways and means of putting it into effect immediately.

But reason told him that if he went back and confronted her now, the way he longed to do, nothing between them would really have changed. Within days—hours, probably—the same old conflicts would surface all over again.

So, what were the sources of that conflict? And how could he best resolve them?

He tried to pinpoint the things that seemed to cause them the most trouble, and what he came back to repeatedly was Elias Redthorn.

Before that particular issue, they had argued; and he suspected that he and Jenny would always argue—with the same fervor they made love. But for some reason, the arguments had become bitter, and it had all started with Elias Redthorn. That case had devolved into a major sore point between them, probably because it seemed to symbolize to Jenny all the injustices she saw in the legal system.

The case had nagged at Zach, as well, even though he was far too proud to admit it to Jenny. The crippled man haunted him, and more than once he'd wished his partners had thought differently about the firm's taking it on.

The logical conclusion, therefore, was for Zach to do something about Elias Redthorn, damn his whiny little hide!

He was snowed under with the final preparations on the Solomen case—it went to court in exactly two days and four hours—but after that was out of the way, Zach vowed grimly, after that, it was Elias Redthorn all the way.

He pushed the button on the intercom.

"Yes, Mr—Zach?"

"Brenda, I'm going to need your help here. I need some files, from the legal-aid clinic. Could you please—"

"Would this have anything to do with Ms. Lathrop, Mr. Jones?"

Zach sighed. "Yes, Brenda. Yes, it would."

"No problem. I'll get you whatever you need. Nice to have you back, Zach."

There was such a thing as being too informal, and Brenda was on the verge. But he realized he was smiling for the first time in days.

11

THE SOLOMEN TRIAL took three days, and Zach had never been as emotionally involved in a case in his entire career. He did his absolute best, keeping a cool and contained persona both in court and outside, where he and the other people involved were besieged by the media.

Judge Munroe handed down his decision late on the afternoon of the third day.

"This court finds in favor of David Solomen."

They'd won. By God, they'd won! Zach felt a tidal wave of relief wash over him, mixed with heady elation. He gripped David's shoulder as the judge went on. "In the matter of Solomen versus Northwest Growers' Association, I award damages in the amount of $100,000 for loss of revenue and loss of opportunity.

"In the matter of *Solomen* versus *Safefood*, I award damages in the amount of $50,000 for damaging the reputation of Solomen Organic Produce Marts as suppliers in good faith of organically grown fruits and vegetables."

Zach turned to look at David. There were tears slowly rolling down the big, gentle man's cheeks, and he was making no effort to wipe them away.

"This court also directs that all of the costs in this action, plus legal fees, are to be borne by Safefood, who initiated these proceedings. The courts are not intended as a public forum. This matter could have been settled without the amount of publicity and public fanfare generated by a court action."

Afterward, David insisted on buying dinner for everyone at a vegetarian restaurant. Over glasses of apple juice, he announced that he and Brenda were engaged.

Brenda caught Zach's eye and held her glass up to him in a silent toast.

ALONE AT LAST, late that night, Zach sat in front of the television staring blindly at the screen. A talk-show host was holding forth, but earlier, the Solomen trial and the verdict had made the local news. Zach had squirmed at the sight of his own face and voice on the screen.

Ken and Derek had both phoned right after the broadcast, exuberant about his victory but also delighted with the amount of money and publicity the firm would receive from the case.

All in all, it *was* a marvelous victory, and Brenda had been right: The publicity was worth its weight in gold. So was winning a battle that he'd felt was morally right.

The one factor that made the whole thing bittersweet was not being able to share it with Jenny.

Each time the phone rang, his heart beat a little faster, as he hoped it might be her. But she hadn't called.

His mother did, bursting with excitement and pride, and even his father had come on the line. "Good work, son," was all he'd said, but Zach could count on one hand the number of times Theodore had said that to him.

Then Serena called, obviously proud of him, too; but like Theodore, she was very cool and reserved about it all.

"I thought I'd ask that young woman of yours, Jenny, to have lunch with me sometime soon," she remarked before she hung up. "Is she there with you, by any chance?"

How Zach wished he could say yes. "No, she's not," he admitted. "We had a blowup a couple of weeks ago. I haven't seen her since," he told Serena truthfully.

"And how do you feel about that?"

"Jesus, Serena, drop the analyst jargon, okay? If you really want to know, I feel suicidal, I feel broken-hearted, I feel devastated. But I've got a game plan here, and I'm going to get her back."

There was a long moment of silence, and then his sister's cool voice said, "I hope you're successful, big brother. I rather got the impression she wasn't one of your usual bimbos."

"Damned right, she isn't. I intend to marry Jenny." He almost added, "Whether she likes it or not."

There was another silence, longer this time. "I see. Well, if there's anything I can do to help..."

He got up after that call and poured himself another glass of the natural apple juice he'd bought on his way home. There was a lot to be said for the stuff. It wasn't Scotch by any stretch of the imagination, but it was wet, it filled the need to hold a glass in his hand at a time like this, and it wasn't going to give him a hangover in the morning.

He tried to imagine what Jenny was doing right at that moment. He figured probably sleeping, on her side the way she usually did, knees folded, arm beneath her head, hair tumbled all across the pillow.

He wistfully traced the shape and feel of her slight, warm body—the small, firm breasts, the rounded hips.

He became hard at the image.

Sighing, he chugged the apple juice down and planned his strategy in the matter of *Elias Redthorn* versus *the City of Vancouver*.

He'd begin the next morning using his success in the *Solomen* case as blackmail with Ken and Derek, to get them to agree to his taking on Redthorn.

He'd work his ass off and push for an early trial date on the thing—the sooner the better.

Because the sooner he got a sizable settlement for Elias Redthorn, the sooner he'd have Jenny back again.

HUNCHED ON HER new navy blue couch, Jenny sat bundled in her old flannelette nightgown, eating a bowl of cold cereal and watching Zach on television.

He was wearing his charcoal-gray suit with a pristine white shirt and the burgundy silk tie she'd undone numerous times. Seeing him made her tremble, and she set the cereal down on the floor, unfinished.

The attractive female news announcer sounded just the slightest bit breathless. "Give us your reaction to winning the *Solomen* case, Mr. Jones."

He smiled into the camera, and Jenny started to cry. That smile had been the first blurry thing she'd seen in the morning, when Zach was with her. She'd open her eyes, and he'd be smiling just like that, propped on an elbow, watching her struggle to wake up.

That memory intensified the loneliness that had grown intolerable these past weeks.

"It reassures me that justice is alive and well and living in Vancouver," he said. It was the perfect thing to say, Jenny thought as she blew her nose on a paper serviette; not preachy or boastful, just dignified and rather...honorable.

She was so proud of him she could hardly stand it.

"That was Zachary Jones, counsel for the defense in the case of *Safefood* versus *Solomen*. Judge Monroe handed down a landmark decision this afternoon, chastising the environmental group and penalizing them financially for what he terms the misuse of the judicial system. I'm Karen Baher, reporting from the courthouse."

Jenny blew her nose again, and thought uncomfortably of all the things she'd accused Zach of in that final, dreadful quarrel.

She'd known he was defending Solomen, and that the case was anything but a typical lucrative litigation case. He'd told her Solomen didn't have a lot of money, that he was fighting it on contingency. But she'd chosen to ignore that side of him.

Why hadn't she been willing to talk with him, discuss the things that were bothering both of them that night? Why had she forced the issue, said things that she knew would hurt him?

She'd been the one who ended it, not Zach. She'd asked him to leave. Why? Why wreck the one relationship in her life that truly was remarkable?

Because she was running scared.

Because her whole life had been a series of failures at loving, she'd been afraid to let herself believe that this time could be different. She'd been scared he would leave her, the way her mother had, her father, Nick—

everyone she'd ever cared about. So she had engineered the final parting herself.

If I do it, you won't have a chance to. It won't hurt as much if I do it myself.

Oh, Zach, my beloved. What have I done to us?

She brought her knees up to her chest and held on tight as the bitter recognition spread through her.

The phone rang a long time later, and Jenny's heart leaped, just the way it always did before she could assure herself it wouldn't be Zach.

It wasn't him, of course. But it was his sister, Serena.

Jenny felt every nerve ending stand to wary attention. She fervently hoped that she didn't sound as if she'd been crying.

They went through a series of stilted formalities, and then Serena said, "Jenny, I thought it would be fun for us to get together for lunch one day this week. I just saw Zach on television. Wasn't he superb?"

Jenny wholeheartedly agreed.

"It reminded me that I haven't been in touch the way I promised. How about tomorrow? Are you free? I'll be on campus. We could meet at that little sandwich shop in the village."

God, she'd rather be guillotined than have to spend a lunch hour with Serena, Jenny thought in a panic. She couldn't keep up a facade of lighthearted chatter. She was far too vulnerable these days to be able to hide her misery for very long. Obviously, Serena had no idea Jenny and Zach had broken up. She wouldn't be wasting her time, taking Jenny's head apart to see what made it tick, if she knew Jenny was no longer a threat to the Jones dynasty.

Well, she wasn't about to enlighten her, Jenny decided. But she certainly wasn't about to strain her already shattered nervous system over a lunch with Serena Jones, either.

"I'm sorry, I can't possibly make it tomorrow." No explanation, no excuses. Who was it who said, Never apologize, never explain?

Silence for a long moment, and then, "What a shame. I was hoping... Well, perhaps another time soon. Give me a call. You can reach me either at home or at the Health Sciences psych unit on campus. Bye now."

Hands trembling, Jenny hung up.

THE FOLLOWING AFTERNOON, she was called out of her final class of the day to answer the phone. It was an emergency, the caller had insisted.

It was Veronica.

She was in jail again, charged with shoplifting.

"Shoplifting? Shoplifting. Jeez, Veronica, what did you go and do that for?" Jenny was thoroughly out of patience with her.

Weeping and stammering, Veronica begged Jenny to come and get her out. The recollection of the last time she'd rescued Veronica was all too fresh in Jenny's mind, and she hesitated.

"Please, oh, please, Miss Jenny. I can't stand being locked up. You know I can't. Please?"

Jenny sighed. She'd have to go. Her conscience wouldn't let her do anything else.

"All right, Veronica, I'll come down. But I have to take the bus, so it's going to be a while."

THIS TIME, getting Veronica released wasn't at all the simple matter it had been before.

The justice of the peace gave Jenny a scornful look and pulled out a file of legal documents. He consulted the computer and drew up Veronica's file. "This is a summary conviction offense, and Mrs. Glickman does have a permanent address and a history of appearing for court, but she also has a history of previous convictions for the same offense—eight of them. Under the circumstances, the crown will unquestionably be seeking a jail term. For this reason, I'm insisting that someone other than her counsel act as surety."

Jenny's heart sank. "But there's no one else but me. Couldn't you allow it just this once?"

The JP was unmoved. "Sorry." He turned away from the counter and picked up a cup of coffee he'd been drinking.

"Could I see my client then, please?"

Jenny rode the elevator to the top floor where the jail cells were. Veronica was brought into the cell set aside for interviews. She was a sad, disgusting mess. Her hair was a rat's nest, her eyes swollen from crying, and her layers of coats dirtier than usual. She was wringing her hands, obviously distraught.

"Miss Jenny, I'm so glad you're here. You can get me out, can't you?"

Jenny explained the predicament. Veronica, her watery blue eyes wild, became still more agitated. "What you've got to do, Miss Jenny, is call Conroy. He'll come and get me out. He's done it before. Go call him. His number's in the phone book—I can't ever remember it."

Exasperated, Jenny stared at her hapless client. Was Veronica hallucinating again, or was she relating facts?

Jenny remembered the property taxes, the checks from a Mr. Clark. She sighed and shook her head. "I'll give it a try, Veronica, but I have the feeling you're about to have me make a gigantic fool of myself."

Downstairs again, she began searching the phone directory.

There were two or three pages of Clarks. But there, between Colin Clark and Cornelius Clark, was Conroy.

Dubious, she tried the number.

"Hello?" The man's voice was low-pitched and gentle.

"Mr. Clark, my name is Jenny Lathrop, I'm a law student, acting as counsel for Veronica Glickman. She's in some difficulty, and she seems to think—"

"Where is she?"

"At 312 Main Street. The city jail."

He sighed. "Again, huh? I'll be right down. Good thing you caught me on my day off."

Dumbfounded, Jenny slowly hung up.

CLARK WAS A TALL, thin man in his fifties, casually but expensively dressed in cords and a sheepskin-lined brown leather jacket. He was obviously familiar with the procedure that released Veronica. He posted bond, and announced that he'd drive Veronica, subdued and exhausted, over to her house.

"Do you have a car, Ms. Lathrop?" There was nothing dynamic about him, but he was quietly capable.

"I came by bus, I can easily—"

"Not at all. Come along with us."

Veronica had regained some of her usual bombastic aplomb by the time they were seated in Clark's elegant black Lincoln sedan. She insisted on getting in the front beside him. She demanded a cigarette and then, drawing deeply on it, regaled the other two with a convoluted tale of how she'd been framed and wrongfully charged. But by the time they reached her house, she was silent again, obviously worn-out.

Clark didn't lecture her, and neither did he flinch when she leaned over and kissed his cheek before she got out of the car. He patted her arm and gave her a weary smile.

"Goodbye, Veronica."

"If you want to come in, I'll buy you both a drink," Veronica offered with a final show of bravado.

Clark gently refused. Leaving the motor idling, he waited until Veronica had unlocked her front door and gone inside.

"Why not move up front, Ms. Lathrop?" His faint, weary smile came and went again. "It makes me feel less like a chauffeur."

Jenny did. Veronica's pungent aroma and the smell of her cigarette filled the car, and he pushed a button that rolled the windows down. He asked her address, and they drove through the evening streets of the downtown city almost in silence. There were a million questions Jenny wanted to ask, but Clark seemed lost in a reverie, driving competently without really thinking about what he was doing.

At a stoplight on Granville, he suddenly asked, "How did you meet Veronica, Ms. Lathrop?"

Jenny explained about the Legal Clinic and the problems with Veronica's house being condemned by the city. She wanted to ask him the same question, but she couldn't bring herself to do it.

Clark nodded at her answer. A moment later, he asked abruptly, "Have you had dinner, Ms. Lathrop?"

Jenny couldn't even remember having lunch.

"Would you consider having dinner with me? I hate eating alone, and there's a place near here where I often go."

He took her to a small Italian restaurant where the management obviously knew and liked him.

Although he was reticent at first, gradually over the delectable pasta and Caesar salad, he began to relax. He asked questions about law school and listened to Jenny's answers attentively. He ordered wine, and Jenny had a small glassful. It gave her courage to ask him the questions that had been haunting her all evening.

How did he know Veronica? What was his connection with the sad woman? What had made Veronica the way she was today?

"Veronica and I were married for seven years, a long time ago, when we both were young," he began slowly. He looked across the table at her for several long moments of silence, as if deliberating, and then he said, "Tell me, Ms. Lathrop, where did you grow up? What was your childhood like?"

"My name's Jenny," she insisted before she launched into an abbreviated version of her childhood. He listened closely. When she finished, he looked at her and nodded.

"Your own background might make it easier to understand what happened to us," he responded at last. "I grew up not far from where Veronica's house is situated now, in the Vancouver slums. My mother raised me. I never knew my father. An old guy sold me a beat-up guitar for five bucks I'd earned shoveling coal out of boxcars when I was thirteen, and by the time I was sixteen, I was singing on street corners."

A smile played across his mouth as he remembered. "I got in some trouble that year, spent six months in a juvenile detention home for breaking and entering. One of the supervisors there took an interest in me, arranged for me to have a few music lessons, and when I got out, a couple of coffee houses hired me to play and sing on weekends for their clientele, and that's how I met Veronica. I was nineteen by then, and so was she, and that's about all we had in common. She was the only child of a wealthy and prominent family. Her father was a liquor importer. She'd had a private-school education and a trip to Europe to celebrate her eighteenth birthday. She was the focus of her parents' lives, and she resented it. Even then, Veronica hated control of any sort. She needed to be a free spirit."

Jenny was fascinated. She didn't want to interrupt him even for a second, and she resented the arrival of the waiter with cups of hot, strong coffee. When he moved away, Clark took up the story where he'd left off.

"We fell in love. You might not think so now, but she was beautiful then. She symbolized all the things I'd never had, I guess."

He gazed down into his coffee cup and gave a small shrug.

"I got her pregnant. We eloped, drove down into the States and got married. Well, all hell broke loose when her family found out. Her father dredged up my conviction. They threatened to disown her unless she had the marriage annulled. When that didn't work, they tried to bribe her, with a car and a trip to Hawaii. Old man Glickman managed to have me fired from the gigs I'd gotten—he knew everybody around town. And of course, I came to hate him and his wife. I hated their money, their efforts to use it to control Veronica and me."

Lost in old, painful memories, Clark sat in silence, his coffee forgotten. Just when Jenny thought he'd forgotten all about her, too, he took up the tale again. "When our son, Derek, was born, they tried to make peace. They desperately wanted a part of their grandson."

He looked into Jenny's eyes and his voice was sardonic. "Now it was my turn to be snotty. I wouldn't let them near him. I had power at last, and I used it. Veronica adored her baby. She asked me to let her parents come and see him. But I wouldn't give in, even when we found out Derek had a serious medical problem. His heart was damaged, and the surgery he needed wasn't available in Canada, which meant it would cost a huge amount of money. There was only a slim chance it would work, anyhow. Veronica told her father, and Glickman offered to pay, but there were conditions—about the boy's upbringing, his schooling. Veronica begged me to go along with it, but I swore I'd raise the money myself, steal it if I had to. Her parents pressured her, insisting she leave me and let them take over Derek's care."

The waiter came and poured them fresh coffee. Clark's hands trembled when he lifted his cup and took a long drink.

"See, she was in the middle. She loved me, she loved Derek, and she didn't want to lose either of us. But she wasn't emotionally strong like I was. She'd been pampered all her life, and her parents were her parents. She begged me, over and over, to accept their help, to bend just a little. But I went right on being stubborn."

He was quiet for so long Jenny began to wonder if he'd say anything more. When he did, his voice was filled with pain.

"Derek died early one morning. The doctors insisted nothing could have saved him, but Veronica went into a deep depression. She blamed all of us—me, her parents. But probably herself most of all."

A cold shiver went down Jenny's back, at the awful tragedy of the situation he was describing.

"It was ironic, but just when my personal life was falling apart, my career started to take off, and I had to be away from home a lot. I wasn't there when she needed me. She started roaming the streets, drinking too much. Eventually she had to go into a clinic. She spent a lot of time over the years in different facilities. That's why she has this horror of being locked up. But each time she was released, she'd gradually slide into the sort of life she lives now—wandering around, fighting, drinking, getting into trouble and out of it again. I tried for years, but she was lost, and eventually I divorced her. I couldn't handle the problems she created."

He was quiet again, and Jenny's heart ached for him.

"Before her father died, he bought her the house. He also left a trust fund for her. She gets money from it every month and will for the rest of her life. Far as I know, she gives most of it away or spends it on booze."

He didn't say anything about paying the property taxes and bailing Veronica out at times like this, and

Jenny didn't mention it. Was it some remnant of affection for that young and beautiful Veronica that made him go on taking care of her? Or was it guilt?

Only Conroy Clark knew the answer, and Jenny thought his reasons didn't really matter. The thing was simply that he did it.

"Did you ever remarry?"

He smiled wistfully and shook his head, looking down at his coffee cup. "My job keeps me busy. I'm on the road a lot of the time—I don't really meet the marrying kind of woman." Then he met her gaze and said in a flat tone, "That's not entirely true. There was a lady, a few years back. I should've married her, but I didn't. Simple truth is, I lost my nerve somewhere along the line. You married, Jenny?"

"I was. He died."

"Well, try again. Don't get stuck in the past the way I did."

He drove her home soon afterward, and she thanked him for dinner and watched as the big, luxurious car slid silently away into the night.

Money didn't buy happiness, that was certain.

Later that night, she couldn't sleep.

She kept going over the tragic story Clark had told her, and thinking of herself and Zach.

Clark had, by his own admission, been unforgiving—just as judgmental in his own way as the Glickmans. Prejudice obviously wasn't limited to the Glickmans of the world. Clark's stiff-necked pride had been the cause of a lot of heartache.

How different were her own attitudes, when it came right down to it? From the very beginning she'd held Zach's privileged background against him. She'd been prepared not to like his family, just because they were wealthy. Why, only a few days ago, she'd assumed his sister was patronizing her with the offer of lunch.

What if Serena was offering friendship instead?

Jenny would never know.

Clark was alone, heading into old age sorry for the things he had and hadn't done, yet unable to muster the courage to try again.

Was that what she wanted her own future to hold?

And what if it was already too late? What if Zach didn't want her anymore? She'd been scathing. She'd said unforgivable things.

In the early hours of the morning, she decided to call Serena within the next few days and ask her to lunch. Maybe, after she'd made friends with Serena, she'd even work up enough courage to call Zach.

A person had to start somewhere.

BY PULLING STRINGS and begging favors, Zach managed to arrange an early date for the Redthorn examination of discovery through the court registrar's office—too early, perhaps. He'd only have a little more than a week to prepare, but if he worked day and night, he might just make it.

Ken and Derek weren't exactly enthusiastic about his taking Redthorn on, and certainly not on a *pro bono* basis. At first they made a lot of negative noises but because of the Solomen triumph, they didn't object all that strenuously.

Zach was the hero of the moment, after all, and he attacked the Redthorn matter with puritanical zeal. He wanted to present Jenny with a happy ending to Redthorn's plight; he needed to hand her the victory as if it were a symbolic bunch of long-stemmed roses.

Zach had Brenda track down Elias Redthorn. The little man was overjoyed at Zach's decision to take on his case, and as Zach listened to him reiterate the details of how he came to be trapped inside the cumbersome body brace, he began to see Redthorn as the epitome of a man treated unfairly by a callous legal system.

Redthorn could hardly get around well enough to take care of his own needs.

Zach understood now why Jenny had been outraged at the situation.

The only real problem Zach had was the fact that he found his client just as repulsive as he had the first time he'd met him, at the Legal Clinic, and the more he saw of him, the stronger the feeling became.

Redthorn whined, fawned and groveled, dragging himself over to the overstuffed leather armchair in Zach's office and collapsing into it with a pathetic sigh.

"Lovely chair, governor, lovely. Wish you could see what I've got fer a chair at my place. Nothin' fancy like this, I can tell you. You're a lucky man, governor, able to afford a chair like this one. Eases me back, this does." He'd lean his head back and close his eyes, his stiff body brace jutting out from under his ill-fitting suit coat, his built-up shoe not quite touching the carpet.

By Redthorn's third visit, Zach was more than ready to donate the damned chair to the pathetic little man, just so he wouldn't have to watch the performance one more time.

But there wasn't time to dwell on personal feelings.

Zach put all his energy, all his waking hours and a substantial amount of the firm's money into preparing his case against the city's Police Department and Constable Marvin Scott, who'd recovered the car and then released it to Redthorn.

At great expense, he hired an engineering reconstructionist to go over Redthorn's car and present a crystal-clear picture of why it went out of control when Elias drove it after the theft. He interviewed all the policemen involved in the matter and subpoenaed them as witnesses. Elias supplied him with a detailed report from his doctor describing the injuries to his back.

When Thursday and the examination for discovery rolled around in the matter of *Redthorn* versus *Vancouver City Police*, Zach was ready. He put on his navy pin-striped suit and walked proudly into the hearing room, deliberately shortening his stride to keep pace with Elias, who was limping along bravely beside him.

Usually, there was a little anxiety about this procedure, a feeling of apprehension about the outcome of these rather formal, pretrial proceedings.

This morning, Zach was free of any misgivings about the action. He had absolute confidence in the essential rightness of this case, and consequently in his ability to eventually win a sizable settlement for Redthorn.

He'd never felt as assured or as philanthropic about anything in his entire life.

He'd never wanted a trial to proceed more than he did now.

He wanted to get this formality over with and have a trial date set, the sooner the better—because the sooner he won, the sooner he could convince the woman he loved to marry him.

The registrar, Mr. John Seaton, who happened to be an old friend of Zach's father, was a dignified and stately man. Conscious of propriety, he met Zach's gaze and gave an almost-imperceptible nod of recognition.

"In the matter of *Redthorn* versus *Vancouver City Police*, Mr. Jones, would you like to present your evidence?"

Feeling righteous, Zach began.

12

SERENA HAD SUGGESTED Thursday as a good day for
lunch, and Jenny was waiting, more than a little nervous and annoyed, when Zach's sister hurried into the
cozy restaurant long past the one o'clock they'd agreed
on. Jenny had spent the time checking the menu prices
and adding up the money in her wallet. She'd invited
Serena, and she was determined she was paying for
lunch. It gave her some obscure feeling of power and
control.

"Sorry I'm late. There's always an emergency just
when you're in a hurry. You're so fortunate to still be a
student and not have to deal with the realities of the
work world."

Jenny, even though she tried not to, felt a small stab
of resentment at that. She thought of her trips down to
the city jail to spring Veronica, and the fact that she'd
cut an important lecture just to accommodate this
luncheon. Now, because Serena was late, she'd miss the
next one, as well. What the hell did this woman, in her
expensive wool suit, know about reality?

She bit her tongue. She was going to be open and
warm and friendly and nonjudgmental. Even if it
strangled her.

But talking with Serena, one on one, was no easier
than it had been with Zach beside her. She was so cool
and utterly poised that Jenny felt like an awkward thir-

teen-year-old being subjected to an IQ test. A not-quite-bright thirteen-year-old.

After several eons had passed as they remarked on how nice the café was, the waitress finally came, and they ordered.

They discussed the weather as Serena nibbled at her salad and Jenny hungrily attacked her toasted tomato sandwich and double order of fries.

Serena hoped it would snow so she could go up to the condo at Whistler and get some skiing in.

Jenny prayed it wouldn't. Snow meant the city buses might not run, so transportation became a major pain, and her basement suite turned three degrees colder than an igloo.

Serena tactfully changed the subject to clothes. Did Jenny know that Elle, the smart little designer boutique in Granville, was having a sale?

Jenny knew the store. It was half a block from New To You, where she'd found some of her best bargains.

Stalemate.

Serena rallied, mentioning the latest prank the engineering students had pulled on campus. A hundred-foot-high balloon, shaped like a condom, was somehow attached to the top of the clock tower, with a fan inside that kept the thing constantly inflated.

Serena thought it was an outrage. Jenny had found it pretty funny.

Jenny ordered a hot-fudge sundae for dessert. Serena had tea—no cream or sugar. Jenny felt like a glutton, and didn't care.

She had her mouth full when Serena set her teacup down and cleared her throat. Her piercing green eyes boring into Jenny, she said, "I understand you and Zach are having some problems. I'm quite good at counseling, if you'd care to talk about it. It's the difference in your backgrounds that's causing the trouble?"

Jenny choked and before she could get her napkin to her mouth, spatters of chocolate ice cream went flying across the table, and through streaming eyes she saw them land on Serena's white silk shirt. Tears ran down her face, taking with them the mascara she'd put on in Serena's honor.

"It's ... it's ... umm ... it's a private matter," she finally managed to gasp, taking a huge gulp of water. And how in blazing hell did Serena know so much about it, anyway?

As if she'd read her mind, Serena went on, unperturbed. "I was talking to Zach, and I was concerned. He's rather fond of you, Jenny."

"Fond?" Had Zach said that, too. That he was rather fond of her? The very idea of Zach discussing their relationship with anyone made her furious. Discussing her with Serena and using a word like *fond* ... Well, she'd kill him for it.

Fond, indeed! She remembered the passion they'd shared, the intensity of their loving, and a fine rage took the place of the empty, lost feeling she'd been trying to fill with food ever since she'd lost him. She wanted to shock this confident, patronizing Jones woman right out of her elegant black pumps.

"Did he tell you he was fond enough of me to break my bed one night, making love?" Jenny heard herself saying in a furious tone to her.

To her amazement, Serena smiled at that—her controlled, cool smile, which Jenny considered condescending.

"Oh, I know the two of you are sexually compatible," she remarked, glancing at her diamond-encrusted wristwatch. "Well, if you don't want to discuss it, I'm afraid I must fly. It's been fun. We'll do it again soon. Good luck with my big brother."

She scooped up the check, paid the cashier and swept out the door, leaving Jenny frustrated, furious, trembling, and feeling betrayed.

Serena could drive a saint to homicide.

And Zach . . . How could he actually confide in that woman, sister or not?

Gradually, rage overcame the other emotions Serena had generated.

Tonight was Legal Clinic, there were things she had to prepare, and the afternoon was almost shot. But after the clinic, she was going to do her best to track down Zachary Jones and give him a piece of her mind.

"Another refill, sir?"

"Sure, why not?" Zach had been in the pub for over an hour now, ever since the examination for discovery had ended earlier that afternoon. The coffee he was drinking certainly wasn't doing anything to blur the scene in the registrar's office, but Zach doubted anything would accomplish that. He still had the uncontrollable urge to murder Elias Redthorn, but maybe that would go away, too. Eventually.

"Thanks."

"No problem." The bartender gave him an odd look. He probably thought Zach was weird, sitting in a pub and drinking coffee, but he didn't say anything.

Zach took a long gulp of the lukewarm liquid, oblivious to the way it tasted.

The entire fiasco kept replaying in his head.

The plaintiff customarily presented evidence first, and Zach had stood with supreme confidence, reading the depositions from witnesses, producing the corroborative evidence the engineering reconstructionist had come up with about the car, showing the statement Redthorn had given him from the doctor detailing the back injuries.

Zach had made a short, brilliantly impassioned speech about the difficulties of getting through life doubly handicapped as the result of a miscarriage of justice.

He hadn't had a moment's doubt about a damned thing until Ozzie King appeared, carrying a video and apologizing to everyone for being late, then taking his place beside the lawyer for the defense.

When Zach sat down, the defense lawyer set up a video machine and from the moment it was switched on, Zach wished with all his heart that he'd become a football player instead of a lawyer.

The first frames were taken at Parker's Billiards, the day after Zach had agreed to take the case. Elias had obviously discarded the body brace and was bent over a snooker table, cue held expertly, a cigar in the corner of his lying little mouth.

In the next frames, Redthorn was drinking beer with his arm around a bosomy brunette in red tights. There was no sign of the body brace, and no indication that Elias was suffering any discomfort other than sexual turbulence.

The final shot was of Elias at the racetrack—again without the brace—limping over to collect his winnings from the ticket window, with a big grin on his devious face.

Mr. John Seaton had, of course, denied trial. He'd questioned Redthorn about the medical report and Elias admitted it was from a doctor he knew who would sign anything for fifty dollars.

Mr. Seaton then fixed Zach with his beady, judgmental eye and lectured him.

"Before you launch into an action of this nature, young man, you should delve deeper into the integrity of your client."

Zach humbly apologized for wasting everyone's time, feeling more a fool than he could ever remember.

He left the building with Redthorn plucking at his suit coat and whining about bad luck, and Ozzie King blaring out, "No hard feelings, right, counselor? A job's a job, right?"

It was to keep himself from shoving Redthorn into the path of an oncoming bus that Zach had taken refuge in the pub.

He'd started to order a drink, then changed it to coffee instead. He needed to get control of himself, and liquor wasn't the answer for that. The bartender refilled the mug twice, and it was almost empty again before the towering rage inside began to calm.

Another refill, and he gradually began to see the element of black humor in the whole thing.

He'd done exactly what he was always warning Jenny against doing. He'd taken Redthorn at face value; he'd believed his story because the man seemed so pathetic, so vulnerable. Why hadn't he checked him out minutely, the way he had Solomen, the way he did every other client he took on?

Zach admitted to himself that he'd decided to be a perfect hero in Jenny's eyes, and to hell with the facts. For the first time in his career, he'd let his heart rule his head.

It took a trip to the washroom and a hamburger platter to prevent caffeine poisoning before it dawned on him that maybe this whole thing wasn't so bad, after all.

Don't you ever make mistakes? Jenny had asked him.

Maybe being colossally wrong once in a while was the way to go with her. Maybe she'd appreciate a flawed hero more than a perfect one. You just never knew with Jenny.

Which was exactly why he loved her the way he did. She was the only woman in the entire world for him—except that he'd never told her that, had he?

Maybe he should go and tell her now. She'd be at the Legal Clinic for another hour.

And maybe he should have one little drink of something stronger than coffee, just to celebrate figuring all this out.

C'mon, Jones. If you're hell-bent on being honest, admit that you need the drink because you're scared. And that that's no good reason for having one.

WITH EACH PASSING HOUR, Jenny's decision to find Zach and have it all out with him became less resolute. The steady stream of people and problems wore her down, drained her, and each time she thought of the luncheon she'd endured with Serena, she felt exhausted and heartsick.

She'd come to the conclusion that the differences between her and Serena really weren't due to money or background. The two of them were simply opposites. They might as well have come from different planets, for all they had in common.

Was that true of her and Zach, as well? In between clients, she pondered it. Maybe she ought to just let well enough alone.

Most of the other students had finished with their clients and already gone home. Even Jenny's flood of troubled people had slowed to a trickle by now, and she decided it would be a relief to just go home herself.

Veronica was waiting until the end to talk with her, as usual, and the only other person waiting to see her was Mr. Travesano, a round, volatile little Italian whom Jenny had successfully defended for a traffic violation in small claims court several weeks before. Mr. Travesano had gotten himself into a mess with the Insurance Corporation, mostly because his English was sketchy at best, and when he was under duress, almost nonexistent. But Jenny had managed to sort it all out and get the charges against him dismissed. She'd noticed him waiting patiently in line again tonight and wondered what new difficulty brought him here.

He came over now and beamed at her, his dark eyes gleaming. "Missa Jenny, no problem. Just I come to say thank-you." He set a large brown paper bag on her table. "This is a wine for you, I make myself. I hope you like." He reached across to pump her hand up and down vigorously several times. "*Grazie*, Missa Jenny. If ever I need the lawyer again, I will come to you. *Grazie*."

"Why, Mr. Travesano, how kind of you! Thank you very much." Touched, Jenny smiled at him and came around from behind the table, whereupon Mr. Travesano moved closer to her, gripped her head between his sweating palms and kissed her—a huge, noisy smack on each cheek.

Jenny's delighted smile froze on her lips. Over Mr. Travesano's shoulder, she saw Zach coming toward her table, and he wasn't smiling at all. He had an overcoat slung over his shoulder, the top three buttons of his pale blue shirt were undone and his tie was loosened. His hair was tousled, his shirt sleeves were rolled up past his forearms, and there was a dangerous gleam in his green eyes.

"Ms. Lathrop, what seems to be the problem here? Is this man bothering you?" He leveled a malevolent look at poor Mr. Travesano. The little man began to back up, away from Zach.

"*Arrivederci*, Missa Jenny. *Arrivederci. Grazie*. No problem, no problem." Mr. Travesano turned on his heel and dashed for the door, where the volunteer was already shrugging into her raincoat. The large, echoing room was empty except for Veronica, who was now puffing her way across the room toward Jenny's desk.

"For heaven's sake, Zach, that man was my client. He brought me a bottle of wine..." Jenny's indignant voice trailed off as Zach took the final two steps that separated them and pulled her almost roughly into his arms.

"What the hell was he doing kissing you? That's what I'd like to know!" He glared down at her. "If anybody kisses you from here on in, they'll answer to me."

Veronica had arrived, and was all for protecting Jenny from Zach. She had ahold of one of Zach's arms and was doing her best to pull him away from Jenny.

"Hey, cut that out." Zach tried to shake her off, but she was tenacious, and much stronger than she looked.

He shot Jenny a pleading look, still holding her close despite Veronica's best efforts to rip him bodily away.

"You want me to go call the cops, Miss Jenny?"

It was splendid being in his arms again, but it prevented her from thinking clearly. Distracted for a moment by Veronica, Jenny suddenly remembered what she'd been mad at him about. It almost killed her, but she struggled out of his embrace and scowled up at him.

"What I'd like to know is where you get off telling your sister, of all people, about us, Zachary Jones?" Jenny put her hands on her hips, remembering. "And what's with this 'fond' business? Did you actually tell Serena you were just fond of me?"

"What the hell are you talking about? Fond? I'm not fond of you, for cripes' sake." Zach was out of patience. He smacked his palm down on the tabletop, sending the box of tissues to the floor. "I love you, damn it all. I'm going to marry you. And I never told Serena a damned thing about us. Well, maybe I mentioned we'd had a fight and I was brokenhearted—"

"He's a raving loony! I'm going for the cops!" Veronica let go of Zach's sleeve and headed for the door.

"Jenny, would you do something about that woman?" Zach was watching Veronica struggling with the locked door.

He'd just said he loved her. He'd said he was going to marry her. Something like organ music was playing in Jenny's heart.

"She's going to have a squad car here any minute, and the Vancouver police aren't exactly amused by me today." Zach was sounding desperate.

"Veronica, it's all right," Jenny called out. "Mr. Jones is a friend of mine. He's harmless."

"Harmless? A friend?" Zach sounded as outraged as she'd been about "fond," and Jenny was delighted. She shoved her glasses higher up on her nose and grinned at him. Now that she knew the truth, she could maybe tease him just a little bit.

Veronica came back and took a stance two feet away from them, her arms crossed on her well-covered chest.

"That's what everybody thinks about serial killers, too, Miss Jenny. That they're harmless. I'm stayin' right here, don't you worry."

Zach gave her a malevolent look, and was reminded of Elias Redthorn.

He told Jenny about taking the case on, and what had happened at the examination for discovery. "Redthorn's a con man, and he made me look like a fool. You should have seen him at the horse races, spry as anything without his body brace."

"Why, that little creep!" Veronica was outraged. "Y'know, Miss Jenny, I never trusted that guy. I should never have sent him to you in the first place."

Jenny ignored Veronica. She was gazing up at Zach, her eyes suspiciously bright behind her glasses. "But you took the case on, after all. I can't believe you took the case. You did that for me, didn't you, Zach? And I was so proud of you over the Solomen victory. You were marvelous!" She walked over to him and reached up, putting her arms around his neck. "Oh, Zach, I'm sorry for all those things I said to you. I was scared of losing you, because I love you, too. I've loved you for so long...."

Veronica made a rude noise. "Don't fall for the likes of him, Miss Jenny. Be an independent woman, here. He'll just up and use you for a mud slide, and he's a lawyer into the bargain. You can't trust lawyers—I mean, apart from you. I know. I had trouble like you wouldn't believe with some of 'em. Take it from one who's been there...."

In unspoken and perfect agreement, Jenny and Zach each took Veronica gently by an arm. They quick-marched her over to the door. Zach wrestled the lock open, and they escorted her out.

"Veronica, we're both lawyers. There're things we have to discuss in private," Jenny told her quietly. "I'll see you next Thursday."

As they stepped back inside and closed the door, they could hear her grumbling about lawyers all the way down the steps. No personal feelings ... All they cared about was the law....

Zach locked the door again and drew Jenny into his arms.

"Now, counselor..."

He slipped her glasses off her nose and slid them into his pocket.

Harlequin
HISTORICAL
CHRISTMAS
STORIES · 1991

Bring back heartwarming memories of Christmas past
with HISTORICAL CHRISTMAS STORIES 1991,
a collection of romantic stories
by three popular authors.
The perfect Christmas gift!

Don't miss these heartwarming stories,
available in November
wherever Harlequin books are sold:

CHRISTMAS YET TO COME
by Lynda Trent
A SEASON OF JOY
by Caryn Cameron
FORTUNE'S GIFT
by DeLoras Scott

**Best Wishes and Season's Greetings
from Harlequin!**

HARLEQUIN

Romance

Take 4 bestselling love stories FREE

Plus get a FREE surprise gift!

Special Limited-time Offer

Mail to Harlequin Reader Service®

In the U.S.
3010 Walden Avenue
P.O. Box 1867
Buffalo, N.Y. 14269-1867

In Canada
P.O. Box 609
Fort Erie, Ontario
L2A 5X3

YES! Please send me 4 free Harlequin Temptation® novels and my free surprise gift. Then send me 4 brand-new novels every month, and bill me at the low price of $2.69* each—a savings of 30¢ apiece off cover prices. There are no shipping, handling or other hidden costs. I understand that accepting the books and gift places me under no obligation ever to buy any books. I can always return a shipment and cancel at any time. Even if I never buy another book from Harlequin, the 4 free books and the surprise gift are mine to keep forever.

*Offer slightly different in Canada—$2.69 per book plus 49¢ per shipment for delivery. Canadian residents add applicable federal and provincial sales tax. Sales tax applicable in N.Y.

142 BPA ADL4   342 BPA ADMJ

Name _____ (PLEASE PRINT) _____

Address _____ Apt. No. _____

City _____ State/Prov. _____ Zip/Postal Code _____

This offer is limited to one order per household and not valid to present Harlequin Temptation® subscribers. Terms and prices are subject to change.

TEMP-91   © 1990 Harlequin Enterprises Limited

HARLEQUIN®
OFFICIAL SWEEPSTAKES RULES

NO PURCHASE NECESSARY

1. To enter, complete an Official Entry Form or 3" × 5" index card by hand-printing, in plain block letters, your complete name, address, phone number and age, and mailing it to: Harlequin Fashion A Whole New You Sweepstakes, P.O. Box 9056, Buffalo, NY 14269-9056.

   No responsibility is assumed for lost, late or misdirected mail. Entries must be sent separately with first class postage affixed, and be received no later than December 31, 1991 for eligibility.

2. Winners will be selected by D.L. Blair, Inc., an independent judging organization whose decisions are final, in random drawings to be held on January 30, 1992 in Blair, NE at 10:00 a.m. from among all eligible entries received.

3. The prizes to be awarded and their approximate retail values are as follows: Grand Prize — A brand-new Mercury Sable LS plus a trip for two (2) to Paris, including round-trip air transportation, six (6) nights hotel accommodation, a $1,400 meal/spending money stipend and $2,000 cash toward a new fashion wardrobe (approximate value: $28,000) or $15,000 cash; two (2) Second Prizes — A trip to Paris, including round-trip air transportation, six (6) nights hotel accommodation, a $1,400 meal/spending money stipend and $2,000 cash toward a new fashion wardrobe (approximate value: $11,000) or $5,000 cash; three (3) Third Prizes — $2,000 cash toward a new fashion wardrobe. All prizes are valued in U.S. currency. Travel award air transportation is from the commercial airport nearest winner's home. Travel is subject to space and accommodation availability, and must be completed by June 30, 1993. Sweepstakes offer is open to residents of the U.S. and Canada who are 21 years of age or older as of December 31, 1991, except residents of Puerto Rico, employees and immediate family members of Torstar Corp., its affiliates, subsidiaries, and all agencies, entities and persons connected with the use, marketing, or conduct of this sweepstakes. All federal, state, provincial, municipal and local laws apply. Offer void wherever prohibited by law. Taxes and/or duties, applicable registration and licensing fees, are the sole responsibility of the winners. Any litigation within the province of Quebec respecting the conduct and awarding of a prize may be submitted to the Régie des loteries et courses du Québec. All prizes will be awarded; winners will be notified by mail. No substitution of prizes is permitted.

4. Potential winners must sign and return any required Affidavit of Eligibility/Release of Liability within 30 days of notification. In the event of noncompliance within this time period, the prize may be awarded to an alternate winner. Any prize or prize notification returned as undeliverable may result in the awarding of that prize to an alternate winner. By acceptance of their prize, winners consent to use of their names, photographs or their likenesses for purposes of advertising, trade and promotion on behalf of Torstar Corp. without further compensation. Canadian winners must correctly answer a time-limited arithmetical question in order to be awarded a prize.

5. For a list of winners (available after 3/31/92), send a separate stamped, self-addressed envelope to: Harlequin Fashion A Whole New You Sweepstakes, P.O. Box 4694, Blair, NE 68009.

PREMIUM OFFER TERMS

To receive your gift, complete the Offer Certificate according to directions. Be certain to enclose the required number of "Fashion A Whole New You" proofs of product purchase (which are found on the last page of every specially marked "Fashion A Whole New You" Harlequin or Silhouette romance novel). Requests must be received no later than December 31, 1991. Limit: four (4) gifts per name, family, group, organization or address. Items depicted are for illustrative purposes only and may not be exactly as shown. Please allow 6 to 8 weeks for receipt of order. Offer good while quantities of gifts last. In the event an ordered gift is no longer available, you will receive a free, previously unpublished Harlequin or Silhouette book for every proof of purchase you have submitted with your request, plus a refund of the postage and handling charge you have included. Offer good in the U.S. and Canada only.

HQFW-SWPR

HARLEQUIN® OFFICIAL
SWEEPSTAKES ENTRY FORM

4-FWHTS-4

Complete and return this Entry Form immediately – the more entries you submit, the better your chances of winning!

- Entries must be received by December 31, 1991.
- A Random draw will take place on January 30, 1992.
- No purchase necessary.

Yes, I want to win a FASHION A WHOLE NEW YOU Classic and Romantic prize from Harlequin:

Name _____ Telephone _____ Age _____

Address _____

City _____ State _____ Zip _____

Return Entries to: **Harlequin FASHION A WHOLE NEW YOU,**
P.O. Box 9056, Buffalo, NY 14269-9056   © 1991 Harlequin Enterprises Limited

PREMIUM OFFER

To receive your free gift, send us the required number of proofs-of-purchase from any specially marked FASHION A WHOLE NEW YOU Harlequin or Silhouette Book with the Offer Certificate properly completed, plus a check or money order (do not send cash) to cover postage and handling payable to Harlequin FASHION A WHOLE NEW YOU Offer. We will send you the specified gift.

OFFER CERTIFICATE

Item	A. ROMANTIC COLLECTOR'S DOLL (Suggested Retail Price $60.00)	B. CLASSIC PICTURE FRAME (Suggested Retail Price $25.00)
# of proofs-of-purchase	18	12
Postage and Handling	$3.50	$2.95
Check one	☐	☐

Name _____

Address _____

City _____ State _____ Zip _____

Mail this certificate, designated number of proofs-of-purchase and check or money order for postage and handling to: **Harlequin FASHION A WHOLE NEW YOU Gift Offer,** P.O. Box 9057, Buffalo, NY 14269-9057. Requests must be received by December 31, 1991.

ONE
PROOF-OF-PURCHASE

4-FWHTP-4

To collect your fabulous free gift you must include the necessary number of proofs-of-purchase with a properly completed Offer Certificate.

© 1991 Harlequin Enterprises Limited

See previous page for details.

5